MOUNTAIN DELIGHTS

WILD MOUNTAIN MEN - BOOK 2

VANESSA VALE

Copyright © 2019 by Vanessa Vale

This is a work of fiction. Names, characters, places and incidents are the products of the author's imagination and used fictitiously. Any resemblance to actual persons, living or dead, businesses, companies, events or locales is entirely coincidental.

All rights reserved.

No part of this book may be reproduced in any form or by any electronic or mechanical means, including information storage and retrieval systems, without written permission from the author, except for the use of brief quotations in a book review.

Cover design: Bridger Media

Cover photos: Hot Damn Stock; Deposit Photos: EpicStockMedia

GET A FREE BOOK!

Join my mailing list to be the first to know of new releases, free books, special prices and other author giveaways.

http://freeromanceread.com

1

I didn't usually go to a strange guy's house for sex. Okay, *never*. Until now. From what I'd been told, Cy Seaborn was a rock star between the sheets, and well-hung. Skilled and well-endowed were important to me, like any woman, I assumed. And a cowboy? Holy hell, I was getting worked up just driving my old Land Cruiser along the rutted drive across his property.

It had taken twenty minutes from town to get to the Flying Z ranch, another five—so far—up the long driveway. The house finally came into view as I went over a rise. The setting was stunning. Prairie grasses were dry now, waving across the slight roll of the land before the mountains jutted straight upward to their snow-capped peaks. Cutthroat Mountain, the ski resort, was on the back side of one of them. The difference between east and west was remarkable. Here, it was quiet, not a soul around. There, once mud season was over, the slopes would open and people would return to their fancy vacation houses, over-the-top SUVs. Lots of rich vacationers.

My cell rang from the passenger seat. I knew the special ring tone, ignored it. Mark had been calling me non-stop, and I'd been avoiding him. My coach wanted me back into the gym to train, meeting with the sponsors, doing photo ops to prove I was one hundred percent after my wipe out.

My knee was better, but my mind wasn't in the game. It hadn't been since the accident, and I wasn't sure if it ever would be again. I'd done a good job not thinking about that. Meeting Lucas, being with him, had certainly helped. A hot guy and lots of sex could do that to a girl. And now there was Cy. The cell went silent and all thoughts about my career did too.

I smiled. This was it.

I pulled up and parked, looked out the windshield at the place. Typical two-story farmhouse, its vintage I guessed to be in the thirties or forties. It had white clapboard siding, a sweeping front porch. In the distance, I could see some other buildings which I assumed

VANESSA VALE

were the stables and several bunkhouses and small cabins. I wasn't here for the non-profit that was run from this place, but for the man who owned it.

Speaking of... a man came out onto the porch, no doubt hearing my arrival. I pegged him at six-two, two hundred pounds, not one ounce of it was flab. His plaid shirt and jeans didn't hide the muscled physique beneath. If tossing hay bales made a guy look like him, there needed to be a new fitness trend. At least a T-shirt that said *Cowboy Strong.*

Overlong dark hair curled over the collar of his plaid shirt, and I itched to run my fingers through it, hopefully when his head was between my legs and he was busy eating me out. I squirmed in my seat, my panties already damp with anticipation. It was the beard though… fuck. Thick and full, trimmed on the sides and longer on the bottom. What would *that* feel like brushing against my thighs? With the SUV off, the interior was getting cold quickly, but I wasn't. Far from it. I was burning up just eye fucking him from thirty feet away.

He didn't approach, just leaned against a post. Waited, with a rifle in his right hand. *Just great.*

He had no idea who I was; Lucas had said he wasn't going to tell Cy in advance about my arrival. Since Lucas wasn't here yet—mine was the only vehicle around—I had to wonder if this was a good idea or not.

The plan was for a threesome… if the third—Lucas—would show the fuck up.

As for Cy, he didn't look thrilled to have company. That would change; at least I hoped. He was going to get lucky, and hopefully fuck my brains out. He just didn't know it yet.

Taking a deep breath, I climbed from my SUV, careful of my left knee, and slammed the door shut behind me.

"You can hop right on up in that car of yours and head out," Cy called. His voice was deep, the timbre smooth like whiskey, and full of threat.

Stiffening my resolve, and my shoulders, I took a step toward him. Only one because I wasn't completely stupid since he was armed and all. I didn't think he'd shoot me...

"I'm here to—"

He held up his free hand to stop me. "I know why you're here. Your kind have been kicking up dust on my drive the past week to get a story. They must be getting desperate if they send the hot chick."

Oh. Shit. He thought I was a reporter trying to get a scoop on the whole Dennis Seaborn fiasco. I knew all about it. Who hadn't, in Cutthroat? The guy had turned himself in for murdering Erin Mills, Lucas's sister. He'd been questioned six ways to Sunday and his story had held. Until a time-stamped traffic camera photo of Erin alive after when he'd said he'd killed her blew it all to hell. Now, he was out of jail—they couldn't keep him for a crime he didn't commit—and everyone in western Montana wondered why he'd stepped forward if he hadn't done it. Who would do something like that? Take the blame for a murder? *A murder.*

Dennis Seaborn was Cy's father. Estranged, from what Lucas had told me. Lucas and I had met two weeks before his sister had been killed, and I was all too aware of how it affected him. I knew all about his friendship with Cy, their working relationship. Sure, Lucas hated Dennis Seaborn for impeding his sister's case, but he didn't blame Cy.

Perhaps he was the only one who felt that way based on the way he was acting.

I looked to Cy, his gaze filled with hatred and anger. Not what I wanted to see there. Lust, desire and need would have been better. From the pictures of Dennis, he and Cy looked a lot alike. They had the same dark hair—although Dennis' was more gray than black now —and eyes. Blood was blood and with them, it showed. And reporters were always out for blood.

"There's been some mistake," I said, holding up my hands, walking closer. We all had problems, and I wanted to forget mine between two hard-bodied cowboys. But I froze when he lifted the gun a bit. "Whoa, you don't need to shoot me."

"Then do as I say." The rifle wasn't

MOUNTAIN DELIGHTS

pointed at me, although I had no idea if the safety was on or how good a shot he was.

"I'm not a reporter."

"Realtor?"

Were people expecting him to sell his ranch and get the hell out of Dodge because of what his father had done? From what I knew, the ranch was huge, extending not only across the prairie I could see, but up into the mountains beyond. Lucas ran his non-profit from the property, he and Cy organizing and taking veterans with PTSD on back-country trips.

"Definitely not."

"What are you then?"

I glanced down at my worn leather boots, then lifted my gaze to meet his, took another few steps toward him. He didn't raise his weapon, so I felt pretty confident he wasn't going to shoot a woman.

"I'm a professional skier. Maybe." I gave a negligent shrug and murmured the last, more for me than for him. "Look, I'm—"

"Whatever you're selling, I don't want any." Clearly, he hadn't listened to a word I said. "Get the hell off my land." He turned on his heel to head back inside.

"Wait!" I called. This was sooo not going as I'd imagined. I'd get out of the SUV, smile at him, bat my eyelashes and tell him his friend Lucas Mills and I were together—and fucking—and we wanted to pull him in on a little fun. A *lot* of fun.

One of my fantasies was two dicks. A threesome with a whole bunch of orgasms to go around. And Lucas had said that Cy was pretty dominant in the bedroom, which was exactly what I'd been hoping for. Lucas was total alpha male, but he didn't push me, and I

MOUNTAIN DELIGHTS

needed to be pushed. I wasn't on the slopes and missed that, god, *focus* I got with that kind of intensity.

I didn't do anything halfway. I didn't win ski championships by lacking confidence. Not in my career and not in my sex life. I knew what I wanted and went for it. And I wanted Lucas... and Cy.

Lucas and I hadn't talked long term. We'd been having fun. With his PTSD, which had woken him up from a nightmare more than once, it seemed he hadn't wanted to commit. Or at least say the words. We'd both been content with just fun. But we *had* agreed something had been missing. And that something was a *someone*.

But Cy didn't want to hear it. Lucas should be here to back me up—he was as game to double team me—and I'd get a double shot of hot cowboy. Okay, so Lucas wasn't here yet. I looked over my shoulder down the drive. Yeah, no Lucas. But I could still charm the pants off Cy in the meantime, couldn't I?

Well… I had on a sexy red panty and bra set, but unless he had x-ray vision, he wouldn't know since I was practically covered head to toe in jeans, a black turtleneck and a light puffy jacket. I barely had any skin showing, let alone cleavage or midriff. October in Montana wasn't the time to do a strip tease outside. With a strong wind coming down off the mountains, it had to be in the low forties, even with the sun shining. It wasn't just the hottie in front of me that had my nipples hard.

"Lucas sent me," I called, hoping that would cool his jets.

That had him turning back. From this distance, I could see his eyes were as dark as his hair. Piercing. Penetrating. As for *penetrating*, I looked him over, took in the thick outline of his dick in his well-worn jeans. *That* was

MOUNTAIN DELIGHTS

what I wanted. He could eye fuck me, but a dick fuck would be a whole lot better.

"Why the hell would he do that?"

I swallowed. Hard. This was what I wanted. Two men to make me forget, to make me happy. I'd shared the fantasy with Lucas, and he was more than willing to fulfill it. If he'd just show the hell up. It was literally time to put up or shut up. I could go down a steep, snowy mountain on two pieces of elastomer ninety-five millimeters wide at over eighty miles an hour without flinching. Telling Cyrus Seaborn I wanted to take his dick for a ride shouldn't be all that hard.

"So you'll fuck me."

2

"What did you say?"

I thought she said she wanted me to fuck her. I didn't have a problem with that. In fact, my dick was thrilled with the idea.

This mystery woman was stunning. Not the typical city slicker looking for a story, she looked Montana born and

MOUNTAIN DELIGHTS

bred. She was tall, probably five-ten. Sturdy like she didn't eat salads for every meal. Her blonde hair was long down her back, straight but thick, and strands caught the wind to blow across her face. She tucked them back without any kind of finesse. It was hard to tell the extent of her curves in her outfit—while her jeans were snug and showed off toned legs that went on for days, her black turtleneck and gray jacket hid a lot, like whether her tits were a handful or full peaks like the Tetons in Wyoming were named for—but I itched to strip her bare and learn every sexy inch of her.

She wasn't beautiful in the traditional sense. She wore no makeup and her approach was no-nonsense. Downright bold as fuck. Hell, at The Gallows on Main Street, I'd been approached by women interested in a little fun on more than one occasion, but I'd never had one come to my front door.

"I said I want to fuck you." Her voice was louder. Even.

Yeah, I'd heard her right. Why would she want to fuck *me*? With her looks and straightforward demeanor, she didn't need an asshole like me, nor did she need to drive fifteen miles out of town to do it. Not with a guy who didn't want to deal with people since his dad's... fiasco, who was turning into a fucking hermit. Hell, who had a dad like his.

Oh shit. She said Lucas sent her.

Was she some kind of gift to get me out of my funk? Of course, she was. What better way to make me forget all the fuckery that had happened than to sink into some hot pussy? And with her? Hell, yes. I could keep myself occupied for hours. Days, even. There were so many ways I could take her I

MOUNTAIN DELIGHTS

wouldn't be satisfied for a long, long time.

I had no problem with this woman leading me around by the balls for a while, and with that bold stance of hers, she'd do it with a reddened ass. She might be in control now, but not for long.

I'd known Lucas for years, and I wouldn't put it past him to try to get me back out there. My father—if he could be called that—had fucked me over once when he abandoned me and my mom when I was nine. I hadn't seen his face since. Until last month, when he'd fucked me over again. He'd turned himself in, admitted to murder. Within days, it was discovered he'd lied. He'd been released, then went into hiding. I'd heard from news reports he'd hunkered down in his shitty little house an hour south of town and hadn't come out.

His photo was everywhere—TV

news, newspapers, online tabloids—and because reporters were ruthless fucks and people today craved juicy gossip, I'd been dragged into the mess. I was *The Son*. The only living relative of Dennis Seaborn, the guy who'd lied about murdering Cutthroat's own, Erin Mills.

They'd tried to get me to talk. I had zero to say on the matter. I hadn't seen my father in almost twenty years, hadn't spoken to him once.

I wanted nothing to do with my father. Never would.

I had no idea why he'd done it. Why the fuck would he admit to a crime he hadn't committed? It made no sense to me or to anyone else, including the police.

But the reporters were like raptors over small prey, sinking their claws in and going for the kill. I was the perfect fodder. They knew I worked with Lucas, Erin's brother. They knew we'd been best friends for years. I'd given them the perfect story on a silver platter.

Cyrus Seaborn: Best friend's sister murdered, father falsely admits killing her.

I didn't tell those fuckers anything, only aimed my rifle their way until they left.

I'd been there for Lucas through the shitstorm, the funeral, dealing with his parents, working through his loss. Still. And he'd been there with me through the fiasco with my father, even though Lucas had every right to hate me for what the bastard had done. Just like everyone else in town.

And since dear old dad hadn't bashed Erin's head in after all, it was important to find out who had, not just for Lucas, but for myself, too. The police had no new leads. Lucas had been keeping me updated since they weren't interested in hearing from anyone from the Seaborn family. I didn't blame them. They had a hard enough job finding the killer without someone misdirecting them. My father had wasted their time when they could have focused on finding the *real* killer.

All that shit was why I had no intention of heading into Cutthroat until the interest in Dennis Seaborn died down. I'd made it three weeks, so far.

That was a long time without seeing a woman. It had been much longer since I'd fucked one, but Lucas seemed concerned I was spending too much time alone, my hand as my only source of companionship. He knew what depression was like since he suffered from PTSD, helped other vets through it.

So, he'd what, hired a hooker? That was a new kind of therapy, for sure.

MOUNTAIN DELIGHTS

She didn't look like one, although I wasn't expecting her to pull up in fuck-me heels, a tight latex skirt and red corset either.

"Yeah, that's what I thought you said," I replied, scratching my beard.

Dust rose in the distance indicating a car coming down the drive. I looked that way, and she followed my gaze.

"Hopefully, that's Lucas," she stated, her shoulders relaxing slightly.

I didn't say anything else until he pulled up and parked. Lucas had all the answers.

He climbed out of his truck, went over to *her* and kissed her. Didn't even give me a chin lift as a hello. He only had eyes for her.

What. The. Fuck?

He gave her a smile, then slung an arm around her shoulders. Then, only then did look to me.

VANESSA VALE

"I see you've met," he said.

"I'm not hard up enough to need a hooker, you fucker," I told him.

His eyes winged up, then narrowed, jaw clenched. "We might be best friends, but I won't hesitate to beat the shit out of you for calling my woman a fucking hooker."

What the fuck?

I sighed, let it out. Okay, so she wasn't a hooker. She was worse. His woman? What the hell did that mean exactly? Girlfriend? Friend with benefit? Fiancée?

I was surprisingly disappointed. I'd wanted this woman, wanted to fuck her as that was what she'd said she was here for, to find out what made her hot so her mind would go blank, so that brazenness would be spanked out of her, softened to just whimpers and moans. She'd be putty in my hands.

MOUNTAIN DELIGHTS

I told my dick to stand down.

Lucas had told me he'd met someone, that she was incredible, that what they had was special. I could see it. They looked good together. I could see the heat and chemistry between them from where I stood on the porch.

Even though she belonged to my friend, I could see being with her, too. She hit every one of my hot buttons, and a few I didn't know I had, and I didn't even know her fucking name.

She wasn't so short I'd have to bend myself in half to kiss her. And I'd be able to suck on her nipples while my dick was deep inside her. But not if she belonged to Lucas.

"Your woman wants me to fuck her. Did she tell you that?"

Yeah, I was a fucking tattletale, but if she was coming on to me, hard, then she wasn't the woman for him and he needed to know that. Bros before hos, although she wasn't a ho.

Lucas didn't freak, only grinned. And his woman? She didn't flinch or cower or even look guilty for propositioning her man's best friend. Her cheeks may have gone pink, but it could have been from the cool air.

"I sent her," he admitted.

He sent her. Huh?

"To fuck me," I repeated to make sure I understood what was going on. "I don't need a pity fuck. That's just wrong."

He closed his eyes for second, shook his head. "You're an asshole."

I knew that.

"Hailey isn't here to pity fuck you. She's here to get fucked by both of us. Together."

Holy shit. Okay, so definitely a friends with benefits thing. Benefits for me, too.

MOUNTAIN DELIGHTS

My dick was rock hard and was pressing painfully against the zipper of my jeans.

"Why didn't you say so?" I asked her on a growl as leaned the rifle against the house. I wasn't just hard as a fucking rock, I was pissed, too.

Why? I had no idea.

Lucas had always talked about sharing a woman. Not a random hookup out for a wild ride, but a woman who mattered. A woman for us to keep. Together.

It had never happened, and I'd assumed it never would because it had always been fantasy.

Until now. Until it was a reality.

Holy fuck.

Not only did I come after her armed with a fucking rifle, but I'd called her a prostitute.

"I was trying to, but you wouldn't let me," she countered.

I shook my head, rubbed my beard again. Fuck, I'd been a total dick. Not my usual MO with women. While Lucas might be the *sweeter* one of the two of us, I was definitely more protective. Ridiculously protective. If a woman was with me, then she knew I was all in.

Not like my fuck-all father.

"Sorry about that. Like Lucas said, I really am an asshole." I wasn't sure if that would cut it, but what else was there to say?

They walked toward the house, Lucas' arm still around her. She looked comfortable beside him. Content. Besides the fact that he wanted to share her—*Hailey*—with me, I was happy for him. It was one thing for him to mention her in a phone call, it was another to see them together, to see how... *right* they were.

Lucas had had such a shit time for so

MOUNTAIN DELIGHTS

long, he deserved something good in his life. Being deployed to Afghanistan had been hell, and while he'd come out of it alive and with his body intact, he had demons. PTSD was a bitch, and he'd been one of the lucky ones, getting counseling and learning ways to cope. He wasn't the same guy who'd left years ago. He was damaged, but he was getting better.

Hell, he was helping others. He knew what other vets were going through, what they needed to cope. With all his money—the Mills were the richest family in Cutthroat—he could have dicked around until he died. Instead, he'd created a non-profit that brought vets to Montana, running trips into the wilderness for therapy. Most of them left from my ranch and rode into the backcountry, using my horses. He'd started something good. Worked hard, busted his butt to give back.

VANESSA VALE

Now, Lucas had Hailey.

He wanted to share her with me. No, she wanted to share herself with both of us. Talk about *giving back.*

"You've had a tough time lately," she said, breaking me from my thoughts. "I can see why you'd be wary of people showing up."

No shit. "It's been difficult," I agreed. "For Lucas especially."

He might not have gotten along with his sister, or with his parents for that matter, but he definitely hadn't wished Erin dead. I glanced at my friend. A muscle ticked in his jaw, but he said nothing, only leaned down and kissed Hailey's forehead.

"We didn't come here to stand on your porch," Lucas said. "Unless you want us to bend you over that railing, doll." He glanced down at Hailey, and she definitely did blush.

"Maybe later."

MOUNTAIN DELIGHTS

Holy fuck. I glanced at my porch railing, envisioned Hailey leaning over it, jeans and panties down around her thighs, my handprint on her ass from spanking her as I took her hard. Yeah, I had a thing for spanking.

I adjusted my dick so there wouldn't be a zipper imprinted on it, then stepped back to let them go into the house first.

"I like this place. Cozy," Hailey said as she looked around.

"Thanks," I replied, closing the door. "My grandfather started the ranch. He built the house a year after he married my grandmother. My mother's parents," I clarified, so she'd know this wasn't Seaborn property. "They handed it down to my mom and now it's mine."

Some of the furniture had been my grandparents', like the dining room table and chairs, some my mom bought back in the eighties. I hadn't updated much since she died except for a new recliner that fit my large size and a flat screen TV. I didn't give a shit about curtains or wall color and most furniture these days was built like crap.

"Want... um, something to drink?" I questioned, but I wanted to ask if she wanted some dick.

"Look, Cy, I'm sorry we told you like this, but I didn't want you to say no over the phone," Lucas said.

I glanced at Hailey, who was tugging down the zipper on her jacket, clearly intent on staying and getting comfortable. My gaze followed the motion, but flicked to Lucas when I processed what he said.

"You thought I'd say no?" No man still breathing would say no to Hailey. "I am *not* saying no."

Hailey smiled at me, tossing the jacket onto the sofa. "Good, because I've

MOUNTAIN DELIGHTS

been fantasizing about this for a long time."

"You want two dicks, sweetheart?" I asked. She'd been bold from the beginning. I wasn't going to change that now.

3

UCAS

I watched Hailey closely. Hell, I *always* watched her closely. Just… looked. When she slept, when she didn't know. When she did. I couldn't help it. She was so fucking beautiful. Intense, fierce. Insanely brave. She was like the strongest warrior in battle, pushing past demons, focusing on the end result. Driven. Failure for her was not an op-

MOUNTAIN DELIGHTS

tion. She did shit only a few had the balls to try. Absolutely fearless.

I could ski. I could hit the black diamonds and back bowls for hours, loving the new powder, the feel of being on top of the world. But I never wanted to race down the steepest of slopes faster than a car on the highway.

Fuck no.

Perhaps it was this intensity for life that I was drawn to. Besides that incredible ass, the one that a quarter would bounce off of. The sassy mouth. The salty attitude.

The silky hair. The full lips. The wet, tight pussy.

It had been all of five seconds after meeting her that I got hard. Six hours later, we'd gotten naked. And once we got in bed... fuck me. She'd been on fire. I'd never had sex like that before. Never knew being with someone so bold could be wild and intense, like it had been the first time. We'd done things together I'd only fantasized about. I was the one who called the shots between the sheets, but she pushed our boundaries.

And that was why we were here now. Getting Cy in on our relationship. Hell, that wasn't the right word. We weren't in a relationship, we just *were.* It was Lucas and Hailey, as if I couldn't remember a time without her. She was mine and I was hers, although we'd never said anything to make it official. We hadn't dated, where I took her to the movies and held her hand, kissed her at her front door. Fuck that.

Sure, we'd gone to the movies once, but an empty matinee, and she'd tugged me into the back row, dropped to her knees and sucked the cum from my balls better than a five-dollar hooker. After I got my brain cells back and dragged her out of there, I'd tied her to

MOUNTAIN DELIGHTS

my bed and ate her pussy until she'd come three times. Only then did I give her the dick pounding she'd writhed and begged for.

We were insatiable, not just in bed, but learning everything about each other. We'd met at a charity mud run in Big Sky, the large ski mountain down by Idaho. I'd been one of the organizers, with the money raised going to various veterans' charities, including mine. Hailey had been there as one of the competitors, her fame helping to draw in race participants.

Perhaps it was fate, or the fact that I told her planned partner I would donate a thousand dollars to the cause if I could take his spot. Best money I ever spent because not only had we slogged through a muddy-as-fuck obstacle course, but now she was mine.

And now she was between me and Cy, ready to take things even further.

Cy and I had talked about sharing a woman before. How it would be hot to claim one together. How it would be safe for her to know she had two men to protect her. I'd just gotten back from deployment and felt my mortality, knew I was broken. If I were going to have a girl, then I needed to ensure she'd be taken care of if anything happened to me. I wasn't enough. Cy had understood and agreed. I needed to know Hailey would be okay, would be protected and loved if something happened to me. I had fucking PTSD. I was broken in so many ways. I wasn't enough for her. She needed Cy to give her whatever I couldn't. After going to war and what had happened to my sister, it was fucking important to me.

And Cy? I had a feeling his own interest in a polyamorous relationship had to do with the way his dad had walked out on his mom. He'd watched

MOUNTAIN DELIGHTS

firsthand how a woman could be destroyed by an asshole spouse. When he was a kid, she'd worked two jobs to support them. They'd had to move from town and to the ranch to live with his grandparents to get by. It was probably the best thing to have that extra family around, too. Still, he could envision how a woman with two men would never have to work herself to death.

And, because I was a kinky fuck, I didn't want to keep a woman to myself, which worked out perfectly. Not just any woman, but Hailey. I'd slept with women in the past to get off. Get in, get off, get out. They didn't mean enough to remember more than their first names, and definitely not enough to share.

The only woman before Hailey who I'd truly cared about was Kit Lancaster. I'd popped her cherry—and my own at the same time, before I went into the military. I hadn't even realized I'd wanted to share back then. Hell, all I'd been eager to do was to finally get my dick wet. That had been years ago. Another lifetime. Pre-PTSD. I'd seen Kit at Dolly's Diner right after Erin's death. She'd been staying with my sister at the time and had been in the house when Erin had been killed. She was caught in the whole mess just like Cy. But, I'd heard she was with Nix Knight and Donovan Nash now and it made me happy to know she had two good guys watching her back.

As for me, everything changed with Hailey. *I* changed. I wanted to show her off, let someone else see how incredible she was. How she melted at my touch, the way she looked when she climbed on my dick and took it for a wild ride. I wanted to see her like that, to watch as she gave herself to not just me, but to another man. Not just *any* man, but Cy.

MOUNTAIN DELIGHTS

I had no interest in him other than as a friend; Hailey kept my dick hard and satisfied, my balls emptied. I knew he'd be there for her. Commit to her completely because he wanted to prove to himself and the world he wasn't like his dad. He'd be able to carry her burdens, because that woman had plenty. She might not have fought the fucking enemy in a far-off sandbox, but in her own way, she came face-to-face with death. Cheated it and survived.

I hadn't known her last winter when she'd wiped out in that championship run. I didn't follow ski racing, but after we met, I saw the footage online to learn what happened to her. Holy fuck, it had been horrible. It was amazing she wasn't paralyzed. Or dead. To understand her debate about returning to the sport, how she was struggling to come to terms with her career, and ultimately her life. She'd been racing since she was a kid. Skiing was in her blood. It was all she knew. And now, it could all be over. What happened to her would haunt me, and if I had my way, I wouldn't let her on a chair lift again.

I was protective as fuck. I was happy to shelter her, to give her the little bubble she needed to figure her shit out.

Not only all that, but with what happened to Erin, it made me realize life was fucking short. Shit happened. Scary shit. Things we had no control over. Erin and I hadn't been close. Never had. She took after our parents, enjoying all the Mills' money; big house, fancy car, fancy clothes and lifestyle. Her little event planning business had been pure amusement to help fill her otherwise boring days. We barely talked and only saw each other for the big holidays.

Yet I was riddled with guilt over not being there for her, to protect her. I

MOUNTAIN DELIGHTS

wondered if we'd been closer, if I'd know about her life, could I have saved her. Now, I'd never know. The fucking killer was still out there. One, once found, I was going to beat the shit out of. Only then could he rot in a ten by ten cell for the rest of his life.

But I couldn't dwell on that now. I couldn't think of Erin, of how her life had ended. Or my parents and how this mess only made them even more fucked up. I had to trust Nix Knight and the other detective to find the killer.

I'd walked away from my family years ago, gone off to fucking war to escape their shit. I'd had counseling to work through every fucked-up portion of my head. I had something good now. I'd built a career out of helping others who struggled like I had, like I still did sometimes. I had Hailey. I was happy. Happier than I ever thought possible. I hadn't told her how I felt, not if she were going to head back to training. She was struggling to decide what to do, to compete or quit, and I wouldn't add any weight to that decision. I wouldn't hold her back, no matter what we felt.

Since she might be heading out at any time for training, I wasn't going to waste time playing games. And thank fuck, neither was she.

When we discovered we were both into a threesome—and not just for a few hours of fun—we didn't wait. Hell, we didn't wait for any kind of sex, and I warned her that Cy liked to be in charge in the bedroom even more intensely than I did. My dick hadn't gone down since I first laid eyes on her, no matter how many times I sank into any one of her holes and filled it with cum.

This mutual desire was why we were in Cy's living room now.

I wanted her. Needed her. I hoped

MOUNTAIN DELIGHTS

to marry her. A ring and a piece of paper didn't matter. I'd even said as much to Cy. But just me being with her wasn't enough. Because *we*—me and Hailey—weren't enough. I couldn't let it be since I was so fucked up in the head. We needed Cy in on it because our happily ever after included him. We had to see how this would work. Long term? Hopefully, but for tonight, to start.

"Two dicks? Absolutely," Hailey said, replying to Cy's question.

My dick swelled at that one word. Her consent in letting both of us have her.

She'd told me she wanted it. Had shown up at Cy's ranch on her own. Had confronted him when he was cranky as fuck. None of that mattered if she changed her mind. I wasn't going to make her. Neither was Cy.

Yet, she was in.

And she might just be the one to get Cy out of his funk.

"You don't even know me," he countered.

"You want to take me to dinner first?"

My lips twitched at her question.

Her fingers grabbed the hem of her turtleneck and she lifted it up over her head, her long hair falling down her bare back.

"Fuck," Cy murmured, his gaze squarely on her chest. "You had that hidden under there?"

I almost swallowed my tongue at the sight of the red lingerie. Cy might have had a rifle, but Hailey had come well-armed.

"I want two men. We've talked about it," she looked to me. "Now that I'm here, that we're *all* here, I need it."

"Why?" Cy asked, his hands clenching into fists. I stood behind her,

MOUNTAIN DELIGHTS

saw the strong line of her back, but Cy saw those perfect breasts. Not too big, they were high and full, topped with perky nipples that went hard beneath my tongue. I could only see the sexy red straps of her bra, but I could only imagine how luscious it looked from the front.

"Why do you want to share me? Why have you and Lucas talked about it? Waited for it?"

"Waited for you," I clarified, sliding my hand along her neck to collect her hair. Slowly, I began to braid it, just like Hailey had said was in that Fifty Shades book. It was silky and gorgeous, but I liked it out of the way. I also liked to hold onto that tail when I took her.

She slid a hair band off her wrist and held it up for me to tie at the end. Yeah, she liked when I took hold of it, too. Once that was done, I moved to the clasp at the back of her bra, unhooked it. I reveled in the feel of her silky skin as I helped the straps off her shoulders and down her arms.

Cy swore again, turned away, ran his hand over his beard.

"Give him a minute," I whispered, then kissed behind her ear, nibbled at the spot at the juncture of her neck and shoulder.

I smiled as she sucked in a breath, knowing that was one of her hot spots.

Her scent filled my head, the taste of her skin was on my tongue, the heat from her body as she leaned into me... nothing sexier than her giving over to me.

Maybe that was it. Maybe we needed to work Cy into it. We'd both had time to think about all of us together. Cy'd had five minutes.

I had no doubt his dick was hard enough to pound nails, but we wanted his head in the game, too.

MOUNTAIN DELIGHTS

"Come here, doll," I said, hooking her hand in mine and pulling her over to the old couch.

I dropped onto it, then settled her between my spread legs. "Put your hands on the back of the couch," I told her as I met her pale eyes. I watched them flare with heat right before she did as she was told. She couldn't see Cy, but knew he was watching.

The position forced her to lean forward, her hands on either side of my head, her tits right fucking there, her nipples little raspberry tips to nibble and suck.

I feasted on one as she tossed her head back, her braid falling down her right side.

"Lucas," she whimpered.

I lifted my hand, cupped her lonely other breast and played. She was so responsive, I could get her incredibly hot just from nipple play. I could probably get her to come, but both of us had been too impatient to find out.

"How wet are you?" I murmured as I kissed my way to her other nipple.

"So wet."

"Show Cy," I breathed, right before nipping lightly, then sucking to gently soothe it.

She reached down to undo the front of her jeans, but one handed, it was hard. I helped her, sliding down the zipper and pushing her pants over her hips, leaving them mid-thigh.

I knew the moment she stuck her ass out because I got a nice mouthful of tit.

Cupping her breasts, I tilted my head to the side to look at Cy. He was standing there, watching. One hand was rubbing over his dick through his jeans, his gaze affixed to her ass.

"Is she wet?" I asked him, tugging on her nipples.

MOUNTAIN DELIGHTS

He grunted, then took a step closer. "Those red panties are soaked through."

Hailey looked over her shoulder at him, her braid sliding down and brushing my arm.

"You going to fuck me or play with your dick like a teenager watching his first porn?"

He stepped close, spanked her, then rubbed his palm over the spot. She shivered and her eyes flared wide, clearly surprised he'd lit up her ass. I'd never done it before with her, but this reaction...

"Interesting," Cy said, clearly noticing the same thing. "That sass normal? If it is, you're going to have my handprint on your ass more often than not."

Finally. Thank fuck.

"Again," she said, wiggling her hips.

"You like getting spanked, don't you?" He shook his head, licked his lips.

"You don't call the shots, sweetheart. You want to get fucked, you do it my way... *our* way," he added, looking to me and giving me a slight nod.

He was in.

"And wiggling that ass isn't going to get it spanked, but it might get it fucked."

She whimpered and her body heated, the scorching feel of it came through my palms as I teased her nipples.

"We were saving that for you," I told him. I'd played with that tight little rosebud, but never fucked it.

He growled, ripped opened his pants, pushed them down enough to pull his dick out. Hard, just as I'd expected with Hailey, hot as fuck between us.

"You go bare with Lucas?" he asked her, his fingers gripping the base of his dick, rubbing it, as if it needed a tight

MOUNTAIN DELIGHTS

squeeze so he didn't come before he ever touched her.

"Yes, I'm on the pill."

The feel of her wet heat coating my dick, no latex barrier between us, was like nothing else. I'd never gone without a condom before. Ever. Until now and there was no going back. No fucking way would my cum not mark her each time I took her. She'd have me slipping from her all day, a constant reminder whom she belonged to.

He nodded, tugged at the dainty strings at her hips so her panties settled at her thighs with her jeans.

"I haven't fucked anyone in over a year. And this pussy, all wet and swollen, eager for two dicks, is going to get taken. Hard. Because that's what you came here for, isn't it?"

She whimpered, her head dropping between her shoulders at his dirty talk. She all but went soft and pliant, as if she gave over to him. I could look down her bare back and see Cy's hand between her thighs.

He'd gotten at least one finger in her pussy and she cried out, shifted her hips.

By the wet sounds as he worked her, maybe more than one.

"Got tested since then," he continued. "I'm clean and I've never gone bare before. Ever. You want my dick, you'll take it bare, just like you do with Lucas. All right?"

She lifted her head to look at me. Fuck, her face was flushed with desire. Her eyes half opened and blurry. Her lips were wet, as if she'd been licking them. Hot.

Needy, and all because of Cy. His fingers in her pussy as I played with her tits.

But this was her call. We'd talked about fucking raw with Cy. She was on

MOUNTAIN DELIGHTS

the pill, and I knew how soft she was, how hot, wet. I wanted him to fill her with his cum, not a rubber. For me to take her, too. To go back to her pussy hours later, feel it coat my fingers, knowing we'd both been there, had her. Marked her.

But adding Cy into the mix meant she had to agree to this as well. Cy's finger slowed, but didn't stop. I plumped her breasts, gently caressed her, let her make the decision that was right for her. He could use a condom until she was ready.

"Okay," she breathed.

Not two seconds after she said it, Cy was working his dick inside her. I watched her eyes flare wide, her breath catch. I wasn't small, and when I fucked her, I took it slow to get all of me into her tight pussy. I hadn't inspected Cy's dick before, obviously, but based on the look on her face, he was a lot to take.

His hands went to her hips, held her still and slowly began to move, in. Out. Carefully. Only when he had her crammed full did he stop.

"You came here wet. Ready. Got the dick you want, sweetheart?" he asked, his voice rough, his breath coming out as if he'd run a mile.

I didn't blame him. I knew how he felt. Her pussy was perfect. Tight. Hot. I bet her inner walls were milking him, trying to take him deeper, mercilessly working him for his cum.

She nodded and I leaned forward, rubbed my nose against hers.

"Good girl," I murmured, then kissed her.

As our tongues met, tangled, mimicked probably how Cy began to move in and out, fucking her with less caution and more abandon.

When she began to whimper against my mouth, I pulled back, dropped my

MOUNTAIN DELIGHTS

hands. She wanted two men, she was going to get them. I got my pants open, my dick out.

"Stop," I said.

Hailey's eyes were hooded, glazed with desire. She frowned at that one word, clearly confused.

Cy did, but stayed deep in her.

"She wants both of us, she'll get both of us," I said.

Cy grinned. He actually grinned. I hadn't seen a smile on his face in weeks. Not since...

No, we weren't thinking about any of that now.

He pulled out, spanked her ass once more. "Turn around, sweetheart, and show me what kind of cowgirl you are."

She looked to me and I nodded. Pushing off the back of the couch, she looked down at how I was stroking my dick, then turned and faced Cy. Her pants were around her thighs. Hell, she still had her boots on.

I had the incredible view of her ass. Taut, full and Cy's handprints were bright pink. Pre-cum slid over my fingers, and I rubbed it in with my thumb.

Maybe Cy read my thoughts because he dropped to his knees and helped her out of everything until she was naked between us and her clothes and boots a pile on the floor.

"Fuck, you're incredible," Cy commented, looking her over, then standing.

She was. Thickly muscled, toned from all her training and competing. Tall, gorgeous.

And all ours. Every sexy inch of her.

4

Hailey

I was naked. They were fully dressed, except for having their dicks out. Stroking them. I turned, looked from Cy, who stood before me, legs braced wide apart, his dick shiny and slick with my arousal, to Lucas, settled in the couch, relaxed, knees wide.

I knew his dick. Knew every hard inch of it. I'd had it deep inside me, my pussy and my mouth. I knew it was silky soft to the touch but hard beneath. Thick with a vein running down the side, it was almost visually brutal, a reminder of how virile he was.

How manly. And now, he stroked it, his clenched fist tugging on the length, working pre-cum out of the slit to slide down the broad crown.

My mouth watered to lick that pearly drop up, to watch as he succumbed to the pleasure I was able to give him.

I didn't want just his dick. I wanted Cy's, too. And what a sight! I didn't imagine he was bigger than Lucas, but it was possible. If I said he was hung like a porn star, I probably wasn't exaggerating. I had to wonder how he fit that thing down his pants. How could he walk if it was hard?

I loved the feel of it as he tried to get inside me. He took his time, slowly fucking it into me and my pussy clenched in emptiness. No matter how wet I was, it wasn't easy. But I loved the slight burn, the stretch, the way he bottomed out because I knew he was all in, that he was giving me everything.

Lucas leaned forward, wrapped a hand around my hip and pulled me back, then helped lower me down onto his thighs so I straddled him, my back to him.

He widened his legs, which parted mine, my feet no longer touching the floor. "Your knee okay?" he murmured.

I nodded. He always checked in about it, making sure I was comfortable, that he wasn't making it bend in a way that was too much. I almost had full range of motion after surgery and months of PT, but it still hurt at times. Still got stiff.

When he lifted me up so his dick found my entrance, it slid in about an inch. Even after Cy had been in me first, he still needed to go slow.

Leaning forward, I settled my hands on his thighs, trying to keep my balance.

"I've got you," he murmured, his voice almost a growl. Both of his hands were on my waist now, lifting and lowering me slowly and carefully, giving me an inch of him at a time until I was finally sitting upon his legs.

The feel of his jeans against my bare thighs reminded me of the differences between us. They wanted me bare, exposed to them completely, while they only uncovered the important parts.

I squirmed a little, clenched down, adjusting.

Lucas hissed.

Cy did nothing but watch.

Lucas lifted me up until he was almost all the way out, then lowered me

MOUNTAIN DELIGHTS

down, gravity helping. My breasts bounced.

"Oh god," I moaned. It felt so good, the way he slid over places inside me that made me hot. No, hotter. Made me close to coming. But facing away from him, my clit wasn't rubbing against anything, and I wasn't going to come like this. Not without some help.

Lucas always ensured I came, usually more than once. It wasn't about if, but when.

"Please," I begged, wiggling my hips, then reaching between my parted thighs to touch myself.

Cy stepped close, pushed my hand away. "Did we say you could come?"

I was transfixed by the sight of his cock, bobbing directly in front of my face. The flesh there was darker than the rest of his body, a darker red, stretched taut. The vein that ran up the length bulging with blood, keeping him hard. Pre-cum slipped from him and mixed with my arousal that coated it.

He didn't say anything more and Lucas didn't move inside me, making me realize they were waiting for a response.

I tipped my chin back, looking up, way up into Cy's dark eyes. His gaze was fierce with passion, but his tone was laced with reprimand. He'd been balls deep inside me, and now he was waiting, dick in hand. His control was unnerving.

I shook my head. "No. But I need—"

"We know what you need," he countered. "We'll give it to you, but when we say, not you."

A thrill shot through me at his dominance. At the control he was taking. How had he known it was something I needed? I didn't have to worry that I'd come. I didn't have to worry about anything. Not about my knee or my career *or even the weather. All I had to do was take their cocks and the pleasure those big beasts were going to give me.*

While Lucas was a lover who took control in the bedroom, he'd been indulgent. Sweet, even. It didn't seem Cy was going to be that way. A thrill shot through me and I got even wetter. I hadn't realized how much I craved his power.

"You wanted two dicks, sweetheart. You can have them." Cy shifted his hips, his dick bobbing right in front of me.

I took the crown into my mouth, licked it like an ice cream cone. The flavor of pre-cum and my own juices burst on my tongue.

"Holy fuck," he growled, his hands settling on my head, then a hand gripped my braid which tilted my head back slightly. "Her mouth's as hot as her pussy."

I looked up at him through my

lashes, saw his jaw clench, the tendons stand out on his neck.

"You'll take both of us, won't you?" he asked.

I couldn't nod, so I took him deeper. There was no way I'd be able to take all of him—Lucas loved when I sucked him off, but I couldn't deep throat like a porn star—so I gripped his base and worked him with my hand in tandem with my mouth.

A spank landed on my ass. Not too hard, but enough to make heat flare. Lucas.

"I don't know if I should be pissed seeing you take another guy's dick down your throat, doll, or if I'm going to come watching you take both of us."

I wasn't ashamed of my sexuality or afraid to talk about it. But telling a guy they weren't enough was a sensitive subject, even for an alpha guy like Lucas. But he'd been on board with a

MOUNTAIN DELIGHTS

threesome, and in a permanent way. He'd even said it should be Cy. But I could understand his current thoughts. He'd admitted he'd never done anything like this before. Neither had I. Imagining it was one thing, doing it was another.

And now the woman he'd said he wanted to marry was sucking another guy's dick. But, he was balls deep in my pussy at the same time. He began to move me, lifting and lowering me, fucking me as he saw fit.

Between the two of them, they took me hard. They weren't gentle, but both were cautious, not wanting to hurt me or push me too far. I felt their restraint and appreciated them for it. This time, it was enough because I was overwhelmed. I wasn't used to two men's voices, feeling two sets of hands, their cocks. Even though it was everything I'd fantasized about, I wasn't used to it.

And yet it felt so good. Lucas knew exactly where to rub and stroke deep inside me. The feel of Cy's cock in my mouth, his hand capturing my braid made me feel so... submissive. My bottom even stung from his spanking. God, I could forget everything, think of nothing but them and how they made me feel.

Just imagining what I looked like, naked between the two of them, two dicks in two of my holes. The feel of Lucas fucking me—we'd never done it reverse cowgirl before—and his ability to watch as I sucked his friend off made me even hotter.

And Cy, so big and thick... god. I felt him tense, felt his fingers tighten in my hair. The way their breathing changed, the sounds they made... the sounds we made together... it pushed me higher and higher.

But I couldn't come. I whimpered,

MOUNTAIN DELIGHTS

wiggled my hips as best I could. Since Cy had told me I couldn't touch myself, I cupped my breast, tugged on my nipple wanting more stimulation, needing more, needing something to push me over. I looked up at Cy again through my lashes, begged him with my eyes.

"Lucas, you said you were saving that ass for me," Cy said. While he spoke to Lucas, he kept his dark eyes on me.

"That's right." Lucas didn't stop fucking me as they talked.

"You might not have fucked it, but did you play with it?"

One of Lucas's hands slid from my hip to settle low over my back, his thumb resting between my parted cheeks. The pad of it picked up some of my arousal and then brought it to my back entrance. He'd done this before, but not in this position, not when he could see what he was doing so easily, when it was bright as day in the room. When Cy could see from his standing position exactly what Lucas was doing.

"Sure did. She loves it," Lucas said.

"Show me."

When Lucas pressed inward, carefully but without stopping, my body gave up any resistance, and his thumb slipped inside.

I groaned around Cy's dick and I swallowed.

Lucas slowly fucked me there as he fucked my pussy, pressing more and more of his thumb in until it was hooked nice and deep, his palm resting flat on my low back.

The slight burn of it, the stretch... the invasion. It was really intense, all three of my holes filled at the same time.

I still couldn't come. I wiggled my hips, but it gave no stimulation to my clit. It ached, throbbed, and I knew if I

MOUNTAIN DELIGHTS

could just rub it on something, I'd come.

"Our girl needs her clit played with to get off," Lucas told him, as if he could read my mind.

"You mean she'll burn hot like this until we decide to set her off?" Cy asked, slowly pumping his hips. "You want to come?" His dark eyes burned into mine.

To answer, I sucked him harder. Deeper until I had to breathe through my nose, the broad head just touching the entrance to my throat.

"You close?" Cy asked Lucas.

"I've been close to coming since I met her," Lucas replied, his thrusts becoming less rhythmic and instead wild, as if his mind was losing control of his body's natural need to rut and fill me with his cum. His hand tightened on my hip.

"Get her off. I can't wait to watch,

then come down her throat. You're going to swallow every drop, aren't you, sweetheart? Or you'll get that tight ass spanked. Maybe even a plug for being a bad girl."

Oh. My. God. No one had talked to me like that before.

I didn't answer because Lucas reached around and slid the fingers of his free hand over my pussy, felt how I was stretched wide around the base of his dick, then moved higher to my clit. The touch was wet as I'd coated him in my juices, and light. So very light.

I jerked, but with a dick in my pussy and a thumb in my ass, I couldn't move far.

He did it again and it was enough. I came, definitely harder than I ever had in my life. Heat burst through my body, my skin was instantly coated with sweat. I couldn't catch my breath, and not because Cy's dick was resting just

MOUNTAIN DELIGHTS

shy of my throat. It was bliss and I clenched down on... everything.

I saw colors behind my eyelids. I heard the guys swearing, felt them fucking me harder, heard their growls and shouts they elicited when they came. Felt the heat of Lucas's cum filling my pussy. Cy came too, his dick thickening right before he did so, thick pulses of his cum slid down my throat. I swallowed again and again to take it all.

He let go of my braid and cupped my chin, pulled back so only the head was still in my mouth. Cum was still spurting from the tip, coating my tongue. He watched as it did so. God, it was dirty.

Only when he was finished did he pull out.

"Don't swallow yet." His thumb stroked my cheek. "Show Lucas what a good girl you are, taking my cum like that."

I was still sitting in Lucas' lap with him nice and deep, pussy and ass. I turned and looked over my shoulder, mouth open so he could see Cy's cum pooled on my tongue.

I felt Lucas' dick pulse inside me as he looked.

"Shit, I can go again right now." He lifted his chin. "Swallow, doll."

I did, then licked my lips to ensure I got it all. I wanted to please Cy. I wanted to be his good girl.

"I'm still hard, and that was the best BJ of my life," Cy said.

I looked back at him, saw his dick was a ruddy red, still hard as could be and shiny from my mouth.

They weren't done. Well, neither was I. I had what I'd come for, and I didn't want it to end.

"More," I said, licking my lips once again, Cy's taste in my mouth. The scent of fucking filled the air.

MOUNTAIN DELIGHTS

In one swift move, Lucas picked me up, turned me so I was lying the long way on the couch, my head by the arm rest. He put one of my legs up on the back of the couch so my ankle was resting at the top, then took my other so my foot was on the floor. I was wide open.

"Look at that pussy," Cy commented. "All swollen and open. Your cum's slipping out, Lucas. Time to add mine to that honey pot."

Lucas stood, moved out of the way, didn't even try to put his pants back to rights.

Cy settled on his knees between my parted legs. Looked me in the eye as he stripped off his shirt.

His chest was broad, his abs like a washboard. There was a smattering of dark hair on his chest that narrowed toward his belly button, then into a line that went directly to the base of his hard dick.

He was gorgeous, so manly, and with his cock thrusting out from his open jeans, virile. I still tasted that virility on my tongue, remembered what it felt like and my pussy clenched in anticipation.

"Ready for more?" His fingers gently slid over my sensitive folds, then slipped them inside. Slowly, he fucked me with them, his thumb rubbing over my clit. "Fuck, you're full of cum."

I was still sensitive, still aroused and I rolled my hips on his fingers. He knew it and just how to get me off.

Again.

"You get two men, you get two dicks. You'll come again and then you'll take me."

I looked down at him, knowing how big he really was.

He grinned, sure of himself. Bracing a hand on the arm of the couch, he hov-

MOUNTAIN DELIGHTS

ered over me, then kissed me. It was so sweet and gentle, just a soft brush of his lips over mine, a complete contradiction to his words and the way he worked my pussy. He lifted his head, and I looked at him. Really looked. He might be the gruff, angry man who'd stood up to me on the porch, but he was also... sweet.

"I'll get all of it in there, don't you worry. You're going to love it."

I came with those words. He was a filthy talker. Dirty. Bossy. I loved every bit of it.

Cy was a man of his word. He made me come, then gave me his dick. Every single inch of it.

5

AILEY

FOOTBALL WAS on the TV and we were on the couch. The couch I would always think of as the *fucking couch.* God, what we'd done on it before they'd carried me to Cy's bed...

Now, I was tucked into Cy's chest, my head resting on his shoulder with my feet across Lucas' lap. I was in Cy's blue flannel shirt and nothing else. I

MOUNTAIN DELIGHTS

wasn't cold, far from it. Besides the fire Cy had started in the stone fireplace, I had two men to keep me warm.

I loved this, being with them. Between them. A safe little bubble. But it was only temporary, or I had to think it was. I couldn't let my heart in on this, no matter how quick I hit it off with Cy. How much I'd fantasized about a relationship like this.

A commitment caused heartache. I knew that from the accident. One minute I was fine, flying down the slope and living my dream, the next I was sprawled and broken on the frozen ground. I'd been committed to my career since I was four. Sure, I hadn't thought of skiing as a career when I hadn't even started Kindergarten, but I'd seen my mom race, wanted to be like her. I loved the thrill that came from racing, from winning. From being the fastest. From defeating an entire mountain and making it my bitch. And now, it was over, or it felt that way.

Yet Lucas had snuck in past my defenses. It had been instantaneous, meeting him in Big Sky at a mud run charity event. We'd been assigned to the same team, spending two miles running and crawling, getting filthy together. I loved to win, but I had been happy coming in second if it meant spending more time with the hot war hero. Turned out, we'd spent *a lot* more time together after, ensuring our bodies were *very* clean, then getting dirty in other fun ways.

We weren't inseparable at first, with Lucas heading off on a backcountry trip and I'd headed to Canada for a promo event for one of my sponsors I couldn't get out of. I hadn't been able to go to his sister's funeral because of it—which had made for a shouting match with Mark who hadn't cared my boyfriend's sister

MOUNTAIN DELIGHTS

had been murdered—but had come to Cutthroat directly after. And stayed. I'd wanted to be here for Lucas, but I was smart enough to remember it probably wouldn't last.

Lucas made me feel safe. Protected. I wasn't Hailey Taylor, the champion ski racer. I was just Hailey. Just... doll. It had been hard in the past to figure out who a guy was interested in. I was a photo op, a famous ski racer to fuck and forget. A notch on their belt, bagging the ski champion. No one was interested in me personally, only what I could do for them.

But Lucas, he'd had no idea who I was. It had been instant chemistry, instant connection. I was happy with him, and that scared the shit out of me. What he made me feel, I craved, practically desperate for it, like a flower in the desert blooming after a rain. While he hadn't outright said it, I had a feeling

VANESSA VALE

he'd be thrilled if I stopped racing, stopped risking my neck. But he didn't give his opinion, hadn't told me what I should do, didn't tell me how I should feel, or act or force me into my role as professional skier.

He was content being with me. *Me, Hailey Taylor.* Talking. Hiking, kissing, sleeping, fucking. Just... being. I liked it. No, I *loved* it and didn't want it to stop.

I felt things I shouldn't. Love would only make me fall again. I'd survived the knee injury, but a broken heart? And now I had double the problems.

I wanted it with Cy, too. Wanted his dominance, his controlling nature. Somehow, it soothed something in me. I wanted to submit to it, to that power. I snuggled into Cy's hold, content.

Happy. *Petrified.*

"Interference," Lucas said to the TV, telling the referee what to call on the latest play.

MOUNTAIN DELIGHTS

Cy stroked a hand over my hair. The simple gesture was comforting. If he were only interested in a one-time tumble, we wouldn't be sitting like this. He wouldn't be holding me, his hands touching me as if he couldn't stop himself. It wasn't sexual, but I was definitely aroused. Just looking down and seeing his big hand caressing my arm—even through the soft material of his shirt—was sexy. And like with Lucas, I felt... special.

"That's a big scar," Cy commented.

I glanced down at my left knee to the straight pink line that ran down the center.

"I tore my ACL in a race last winter."

"Lucas mentioned you're a pro skier."

Lucas huffed out a laugh, squeezed my foot. "You've never heard of her?"

"Other than what you've told me?" Cy asked. "Nope."

The way I was sitting, I couldn't see Cy's face, but I couldn't miss the surprise on Lucas'. He grabbed his cell, swiped the screen a few times. "Here." He handed it to Cy.

The game went to commercial and Lucas reached for his beer on the coffee table. I followed Cy's online research of me, his finger swiping from article to article, playing a few videos. The last one—I'd seen a million times—was of my accident at the championship in Norway and thankfully the sound was off. I had the commentator's words of my accident memorized. Not only could I see the wipeout in my head from when it happened, but also from every angle captured by the TV cameras.

"How fast were you going?" he asked, his voice dropping an octave.

"Seventy-two just before the turn."

I felt his chest rumble, and he tossed

the cell to Lucas when the video got to the part where they lifted me, unconscious, onto a stretcher.

Before I realized what he was doing, he tugged me up so I was sitting on his lap and he was tipping my chin up to look at him. Then his eyes flared wide in panic. "Sorry, does this hurt your knee?"

He was about to lift me off him, but I stopped him by placing my hand on his chest. "It's fine. It doesn't hurt now, nor much in general, I just can't get full range of motion in the knee yet. It's almost there with continued PT."

In his dark gaze, gone was the anger from earlier. The heat was gone, too.

He settled, sighed. "Fuck, woman. You're insane. You're lucky you're not dead."

"It wasn't my first fall," I replied. I'd been wiping out since I was four. It was the worst though and he was right, I

VANESSA VALE

could have died. The knee was the worst of the damage I'd received. A broken rib, tons of bruising. Mild concussion.

"That makes it even worse," he grumbled. "How do your parents handle it?"

I looked at him, saw the soft smile, felt the way his hand caressed my repaired knee.

I shrugged. "My mom skied in the Olympics. She knows what it's like, although we go faster these days. Fall harder. My dad's pretty chill since he's got two women in his life who are risk takers."

"I think he and I are going to get along pretty well," Cy commented.

I thought of him with my dad, fishing, something quiet and calm made me smile. Yeah, they'd definitely get along.

Lucas shifted, slid a hand down my

MOUNTAIN DELIGHTS

back, cupped my butt. "He wants to meet the parents. That's a good sign."

It was. It seemed to be as instantaneous with Cy as it had been with Lucas. Lucas had been right about the three of us. I could feel it, and that was scary. This was all fun. Nothing more. They'd never meet my parents. This... thing wasn't like that. It couldn't be.

My cell went off again. "Shit," I whispered, sighing. The little bubble burst.

"What?"

I pursed my lips. "It's my coach, Mark. He has his own ring tone." A snippet of *We Are The Champions* by Queen.

Lucas leaned forward to grab it for me off the coffee table.

I held up my hand to stop him. "Don't. I know what he wants."

Cy turned my face back to his with a finger beneath my chin.

"You don't seem happy to talk to him. Did he do something? Do we need to beat him up for you? Kill him? I have a lot of land to hide a body."

I smiled, but felt a thrill of pleasure at his words. That he would do something like that, even joking, made me feel good. "He's just itching for me to get to pre-season training. Winter's coming and he wants me ready for the first competition."

"You don't want to go?"

I gave a slight shrug, looked down at his shirt, the way it was closed by only a single button. I circled my finger over the dark hair on his chest that peeked out. "I'm happy here. Not thinking about it."

I glanced up at Cy, who was watching me closely. Everything I said was true. This ranch was an escape. I didn't have to make decisions, just fuck.

MOUNTAIN DELIGHTS

The corner of his mouth tipped up. "You want to hide out here?"

I smiled then. "Like you?"

Lucas laughed. "She's got you all figured out, you fucker."

Cy grinned, but cupped my ass and gave it a little squeeze, reminding me of how he'd spanked me earlier for my sass. "You have no work, no responsibilities right now?"

I shook my head, bit my lip. I should be training hard. Running, lifting weights to get in tip-top shape for the upcoming season. But I didn't want to and ignoring Mark was proof of that. I did have to go to PT. I wouldn't skip on that, on making a full recovery just to avoid getting back to work. It was October. I had time. Or that was what I told myself.

"Just to keep two men sexually satisfied," I replied.

His dick swelled as it pressed against my hip.

"I like the sound of that."

Lucas sighed. "We have to get going. I'm helping my parents empty Erin's house. Hailey said she'd come."

"Besides being your sex slave, Hailey's your buffer with your folks?" Cy asked.

Lucas looked to me, met my gaze. "Damn straight. She's rich and famous. They love her."

I was both, earning enough prize and sponsorship money to live comfortably. Lavishly, if I wanted. And I was famous, at least in Cutthroat Mountain circles, and that included Mr. and Mrs. Mills. I'd met them a few times over the past few weeks and they'd gushed all over me like crazy fans. I wasn't sure if they liked me because I was famous or because a famous person was with their son. Either way, I

MOUNTAIN DELIGHTS

didn't care. After what Lucas told me about them, I didn't feel the need to make them happy.

Cy stood, scooping me up and holding me to his chest as he did so. I gasped and clung to his neck. "Cy!"

"Your parents are cockblockers. She's here to fuck, so we're going to fuck. Lucas, you can have her. Later. I'll bring Hailey to Erin's house, and we can both help with the moving." He started walking to his room. "First though, I want another sample of her honey pot. You'll let my big cock in you, won't you, sweetheart? Or do you want a spanking first?"

6

UCAS

When my mother had called to ask for my help in packing up Erin's things since they were selling her house, I'd stupidly thought they'd actually need it. I'd said yes because of Erin, because I didn't think it would be easy to go through her things.

But when I pulled up to Erin's

MOUNTAIN DELIGHTS

house, there was a huge moving truck in the driveway. Two men were carrying a leather couch up the metal ramp and into the back. Another came out the front door with a large box.

I said hello, but stayed out of their way, heading inside to find my parents. They were in the kitchen, high ball glasses in hand. I could tell by the type of glass that my mother was drinking alcohol, her travel liquor case open on the granite counter by the fridge indication she'd made herself her usual Manhattan. My father had whiskey, neat. It was only three o'clock, but to them it was always five o'clock somewhere.

"Darling," Mother crooned, coming over to set her hand on my chest and buss my cheek. I looked over her shoulder at my dad, who nodded his hello. He'd never been affectionate.

She stepped back and took a sip of

VANESSA VALE

her drink. Yup, the lovey-dovey mother moment was over.

I turned, looked out into the great room where the movers were rolling up the carpet. The carpet on which Erin had been murdered. I assumed it had been professionally cleaned after the crime scene team had finished.

"I thought you needed my help," I said.

This was a waste of time. Why I ever imagined my mom in jeans and an old t-shirt packing a box all weepy-eyed over sentimental things was beyond me. Keith and Ellen Mills didn't get their hands dirty. Not when someone else could do it for them.

"Oh, we do," she added. "We need you to drive Erin's car to the guest house. We'll let anyone visiting use it."

I looked down at the wood floor, set my hands on my hips. They didn't give a shit about Erin's car. The expensive

MOUNTAIN DELIGHTS

SUV was irrelevant to them, that if they donated it to charity they could help people. Hell, I could use it for mine, shuttling vets to and from the airport. But the idea never occurred to them.

"What do you want, Mom?" I asked when I could finally look at her again.

Her perfectly sculpted brow winged up. For sixty, she looked good. Too good. While she hadn't said it outright, I had a feeling one of her winter trips to Palm Springs involved a stop off at a plastic surgeon. Her hair didn't have a hint of gray. Her makeup was subtle but perfect. Her perfume, the one she'd worn forever, was expensive and cloying. She wasn't dressed to move furniture and clean out a fridge. She was dressed for a shopping trip in New York.

Since she thought she was better than everyone else, she had to dress that way, too.

VANESSA VALE

"Want? I have to want something to see my son? My only... remaining child?"

I didn't doubt she grieved for Erin. She might be ruthless, but she was a mother. And Erin had been her baby. The perfect child. Towed the Mills line. Yet she didn't shed a tear, only used Erin's death to guilt me with something.

"You asked me here to help you move. You don't need it. So why am I here?"

Dad came around the center island and stood beside Mom. Side by side, they were a unit, a fortified wall that had always found me lacking.

"Son, you go off for days at a time. No one knows where you are, what you're doing. Like when Erin... well, you were nowhere to be found. We worry."

They worried? Only that I would do something to tarnish the Mills name.

MOUNTAIN DELIGHTS

"I go out on trips into the wilderness. There's no phone reception. You remember the company I run; that I help other vets? When Erin was killed, I was off scouting a new location, planning a special itinerary for those who are missing a leg, who might not be able to climb a damned mountain."

I'd returned after three days in the backcountry to a cell phone with a full inbox and a dead sister. I'd been questioned by Nix Knight, and my story had been checked. The idea they even considered I might have killed my sister pissed me off, but they'd been doing their jobs.

Dad waved his hand, tucked it into his pressed khakis. Mom was in an outfit of pale blue, Dad in a darker shade so they matched.

"We didn't know that! After what happened, we don't know what you might do. It's not safe for you."

"What happened?" I countered. I took a deep breath, let it out, counted to ten.

They waited. Watched for me to freak out. I wanted to. Oh, fuck did I want to. But it would only prove their point.

"What *happened* was I went to war. You know, the fight against terrorists. Bad guys. The one that's still going on in Afghanistan?"

Dad offered me a patronizing smile. "But when you got home, how you had a breakdown."

I closed my eyes for a moment. "PTSD. I had an episode." More than one, but *what happened* was the one they'd witnessed. The freaking out. The violence. The anger. "I went into therapy. Got help. Still getting it, actually. Now I help others."

When I returned, depression had kicked in. I jumped at loud noises. I

MOUNTAIN DELIGHTS

didn't sleep. Considered suicide. It had been rough. Still was at times, especially in the middle of the night. Cy had been there for me. He'd been the one to first take me off camping, riding his horses into the backcountry and let me just be. It had made a difference for me, and now he and I together were making a difference for others.

"You went astray long before that… episode," he added.

Mom nodded. "That's right. You took up with Kit Lancaster." She sniffed.

"Jesus, Mom," I muttered. Un-fuck-ing-believable.

"She was trouble from the very beginning."

"Careful! That's worth more than your salary," Dad shouted, pointing to one of the movers. I turned, looked over my shoulder at how they were struggling with an abstract painting that had been over the fireplace. It was supposed to be of the Montana prairie, but it looked like a kindergartner's finger-painting project to me.

"Yes, you've mentioned how much you dislike Kit. She wasn't trying to steal my money, remember."

"Are you sure about that? She used her body like a weapon."

Yeah, she had. But Mom was insinuating she was a slut or something to get what she wanted in trade for sex. Kit had been a fucking virgin. Hell, so had I. For a few weeks there, she *had* used her body to lure me in. I'd been nineteen, just got inside a pussy for the first time and I hadn't wanted out.

"And when she broke up with me, I went as far away from her as I could. Remember, war?"

We'd had a good thing, but it had ended. I'd needed to get away, from more than just Kit. From my parents

MOUNTAIN DELIGHTS

and their constant pressure to be something I wasn't. From Cutthroat.

Mom pursed her lips. "You weren't supposed to enlist. You were supposed to settle down with someone else."

I studied her closely. "What are you saying?"

"Nothing," Mom replied.

"Nothing," I repeated. "I wasn't supposed to enlist when we broke up? You had a plan for me?"

She looked to Dad. "To take your spot in the family business."

"And Kit held me back how?"

"Think of the grandchildren! Her mother is crazy."

I knew all about Kit's mother and her hoarding, her agoraphobia. I didn't give a shit about that. Kit was sweet. Kind. She'd been great. Back then, I'd thought I loved her, and perhaps in a teenager's way, I had. But grandkids? Kit hadn't ever had sex before. I highly doubted she'd thought about making babies. Then, or maybe even now.

"What did you do?" I asked, my voice low.

"Nothing," she said once more.

I spun on my heel, went into the great room. All the furniture was gone, only a few boxes were stacked in the corner, a standing lamp by the windows. This was all that was left of Erin's life. She'd bought the house with her trust fund money, getting advice from our parents on the right neighborhood, the right furniture.

They were never going to change. I'd accepted it long ago. Hell, I'd gone off to fucking war to get away from them. I was twenty-seven years old, and they still talked about a girlfriend from almost a decade ago. A girlfriend I was suspecting had never broken up with me, that my parents had been involved somehow.

MOUNTAIN DELIGHTS

They hated Kit. They hated I'd gone to war. They hated my career choice. That I didn't touch my trust fund or live the expected Mills lifestyle. Of everything I did. Everything was wrong.

"What are you doing with Erin's things?" I asked, instead of telling them to fuck off. Instead of words, I'd been telling them that with everything I'd done since I turned twenty.

"The guest house. The furniture there needs an update."

The guest house was five thousand square feet and had a movie theater and indoor pool. I doubted it needed any kind of upgrade. The fact that they were emptying out their daughter's house without even shedding a single tear, relegating her things to furnish a home for visitors... it showed a coldness that made me ache for Hailey. For the closeness we shared. The feeling of belonging.

Because if they were this unfeeling about the child who they loved, then I could only imagine how they'd have been if something had happened to me. Like a rummage sale out on the front lawn.

I walked over to a filled trash bag, glanced into the open top. Reaching down, I grabbed out the skull jewelry box I'd given to Erin when I was ten.

"That's going in the trash," Mom called. "Silly junk."

I stared at the jewelry box. It wasn't worth anything, just a piece of plastic that told the time, but I'd gotten it from the back of a cereal box when the *Pirates of the Caribbean* movie had been in the theaters. Erin had seen it and wanted it so bad, being the only girl who had a scary skull to hold her earrings. I'd gotten it for her, mailed in the cereal labels and money, then waited weeks for it to arrive. I'd surprised her with it

MOUNTAIN DELIGHTS

and it had been the one—and probably only thing—that connected us.

The fact that she'd kept it all this time made my heart ache, made me realize there was a piece of her that still connected to me. She hadn't shown it, hadn't put any effort into a sibling relationship, but the stupid skull jewelry box? It said so much.

No fucking way was it going in the trash.

"Hello!"

I looked up at the sound of Hailey's voice from the open doorway. All the anger, the frustration went away at the sight of her. She had on a pair of cargo pants with sneakers and her gray coat. Her hair was pulled back into a sloppy bun. She looked ready to help move.

Yeah, I loved her. Fuck, did I. My dick agreed, perking up at just the sound of her voice. I remembered what we'd done earlier. Christ, it had been hot. And watching Cy carry her off to his room, to hear her cries of pleasure as I took a shower and got ready to leave, to know she was getting thoroughly fucked... I shifted my cock in my pants to a more comfortable position.

I had to tell her. I had to say the words. But what if I failed her? I had no doubt I would. Thank fuck Cy was with her, too. Now, and hopefully always.

My parents came out of the kitchen, their drinks abandoned on the counter, to greet her. They offered her hugs and air kisses like she belonged.

She belonged with me. And Cy, who stood behind her and shook my dad's hand.

Cy was all too familiar with my family dynamics, and it amazed me that they were civil with him, let alone allowing him into Erin's house. What the fuck was up with that?

MOUNTAIN DELIGHTS

If they still held a grudge against Kit Lancaster for doing nothing but being herself, then I would have assumed they'd shoot Cy on sight for what his dad had done. They were the first to think that blood tainted blood and Mr. Seaborn had falsely admitted to killing Erin, their beloved daughter. But no, they still liked him just fine.

Whatever. I was done trying to figure them out.

Hailey came over to me, went up on her tiptoes and gave me a kiss. "Hey," she whispered. "Why are your parents nice to Cy? Shouldn't they hate him because of his dad?"

I looked to where Dad and Cy were talking, my mother walking outside to yell at the movers.

I shook my head. "I was thinking the same damned thing. I swear, I'll never understand them."

"They like me," she replied. The tone was far from smug, only stating a fact.

I nodded. "They do."

"They can tell their golf buddies their son is dating a famous skier."

I nodded, then kissed her temple. "That they can. It works for me. I tell people in the checkout line I'm fucking a famous skier."

She rolled her eyes and punched me in the arm. I couldn't help but laugh. "What? It's true."

"Lucas," my dad called. We looked his way.

"Cy here says he's with Hailey, too."

"What?" Mom practically screeched as she came through the doorway and overheard.

I looked at Hailey, who didn't seem the least bit bothered. Thank fuck. I didn't plan to keep our relationship with her a secret, but I didn't expect Cy to tell my parents. They were assholes

MOUNTAIN DELIGHTS

and she didn't need any of their ass-hole-ness aimed her way.

"That's right. She's mine and Cy's," I told them.

"Actually, Mr. and Mrs. Mills," Hailey said, setting her hand on my arm, giving it a squeeze. "Lucas and Cy are mine. I want them both."

I'd said the same damned thing, but coming from Hailey, they believed it because Mom quickly shut the front door, barring the movers from finishing their job.

"You can't be serious," she hissed, her eyes darting from Cy to me. "*Both* of you? What will people say?"

"That I'm lucky to have two wild mountain men for my own?" Hailey suggested.

"What kind of man are you? Certainly not a Mills," Dad snarled. His face was splotchy, a vein bulged at his temple. "First taking up with that slut, Kit, then going to war. I mean, really. Let other guys save the world. You just needed to settle down and take over the family business. But needing Cy because you're not enough for a woman on your own? A Mills man is supposed to be better than everyone else, not half."

I stilled, barely breathed. I knew how my parents felt about me, but the venom they were spewing now was poisonous and it would take me down, just as they wanted. If my parents thought like this, then it was a good thing Hailey had Cy, too. I'd known they were right because that was what I'd been telling myself all along. I was broken, and I couldn't give Hailey everything alone.

"Actually, Mr. Mills, trust me, Lucas is *all* man," Hailey said, her chin tipped up, her voice full of sass. "I can assure you his dick is magic. I might be a fa-

MOUNTAIN DELIGHTS

mous ski racer, but I'm greedy and like two men who know what they're doing."

Cy smothered a laugh by coughing.

Hailey looked up at me. "It doesn't seem like they need any help moving. Want to head out?"

I looked into those gorgeous blue eyes. I saw anger and laughter, heat and sass in their depths and wondered how pink her ass still was, if Cy had spanked her more after I'd left. My parents didn't faze her. Not one bit. Did I want to come? Hell, yes. Deep in her pussy and my dick agreed.

7

"I THOUGHT you didn't want to be in town," Lucas grumbled as he walked up. Neither of us had wanted to leave a vehicle at Erin's house where we might run into his parents again, so we'd both driven, meeting downtown in front of the bar.

He was in a shitty mood, and I didn't blame him. He was used to his parents dicking him around, but his dad saying he was less than a man for sharing a woman? Fuck, I hated that asshole.

"I don't," I replied, opening the door, music from the jukebox blasting us along with the warm air. "But after that shit show, we need beer and I'm hungry. I'm sick of my own cooking."

Hailey went in first, and I eyed her ass. Fuck, did it still have my handprint on it? I remembered the feel of her pussy as it milked my dick, then the feel of her hot mouth as she sucked me dry. Fuck, I was getting hard. "I figure with Hailey famous like she is, everyone will be focused on her, not the son of Dennis Seaborn," I added.

That was a complete lie, but I was running with it. Lucas needed people around him to feel better. Normal people to remind him that his parents were a fucking disaster, not everybody else. Yeah, I was a total hypocrite, because my own father was the biggest loser.

Lucas needed music. Beer. Bar food.

As for me, it was doubtful any reporters were lying in wait. It had been a few weeks since my dad pulled his shit, and there had been no updates on the case. I doubted there were any reporters outside of the local paper still in town.

Even so, I liked having Lucas and Hailey as a buffer if someone did approach. Since Lucas had lost his sister, I doubted they'd be dicks and fuck with the grieving family. They had some standards... I hoped.

The Gallows did a steady dinner business and got crowded later in the evening, especially on the weekend. But at four o'clock, the hostess led us to a booth right away. I sat across from Lucas and Hailey.

This day had been crazy. I'd woken

MOUNTAIN DELIGHTS

up alone, as usual. Cranky, as usual. Then this blonde-haired vixen showed up and told me she wanted me to fuck her. And I did, not once, but twice, my handprint a bright pink on her gorgeous ass as I did so. My dick should have been satisfied, my balls empty, but damned if I didn't get hard just looking at her across the table. We'd taken her bare. Our cum was in her. Fuck, probably slipping out, making her panties all slick and wet.

Shit. I shifted in my chair.

"Is that Eddie Nickel?" Hailey asked, glancing across the room to a large group that was by the dart boards and pool tables. Based on the number of empty glasses and plates scattered around them, they'd been here for a while.

Lucas set his forearms on the table and leaned forward, looking in that direction. "Yeah, he's wrapping up a film shoot. Probably his film crew taking a break."

"I didn't know he was in town," I replied.

Eddie Nickel was a famous movie star who lived in Cutthroat, at least when he wasn't in LA, which wasn't too often. He had two kids, Poppy and Shane, who weren't into acting or the outrageous movie star lifestyle that swirled around their dad. We'd grown up with both who'd been pretty much raised by a nanny. Shane was our age and we'd hung out with him in high school.

"That's because you've turned into a fucking hermit," Lucas countered.

The waitress arrived before I could say anything. We ordered wings and a pitcher of beer.

"He's shorter than I thought," she said, still looking the guy's way. Seeing the famous Eddie Nickel wasn't all that

MOUNTAIN DELIGHTS

exciting to me, just someone who put his pants on one leg at a time like everyone else. I'd met him before. He was totally full of himself and was pretty much an absentee dad. And since I had one of those of my own, that was one strike against the guy. A big one.

But, bringing a film shoot to Cutthroat helped the economy, so I couldn't hate his guts... much.

"Women toss themselves at him, or at least that's what the tabloids say," Lucas replied.

Hailey turned and looked at Lucas, pale brow raised. "You read the tabloids?"

Lucas flushed, then grinned sheepishly. "Gotta do something while waiting in the checkout line."

A full pitcher and three frosty glasses were placed on the table, and I thanked the waitress. I poured, pushing the first one to Lucas. "You've earned the first beer."

He looked to me, then gave me the finger. He lifted his glass and when Hailey and I had ours, he toasted. "To loving parents."

I didn't miss the sarcasm one bit. I was damned happy I had him as a friend. I couldn't get—or at least keep—a woman like Hailey on my own. Who'd want Dennis Seaborn's son?

I looked to Hailey. Her tongue darted out to lick her upper lip. "What?"

"You know about Lucas' parents. You've heard about my dad."

And she'd still let me spank her ass.

She nodded. "Lucas told me and well, I've seen the news."

Who hadn't? The fact that he'd been a total douche canoe and admitted to a crime he hadn't committed, one as heinous as killing Lucas' sister, should have been enough to have her fleeing

MOUNTAIN DELIGHTS

from my presence, not intentionally showing up at the ranch. She'd shown up for me. Me.

"Fucking insane," I said, confirming what we all knew. "We still don't know why he did it. As far as I know, he's never even met Erin before."

"Why don't you go ask him?" She cocked her head, patiently waited for my answer. Inside, I fumed. I hadn't seen the fucker since the night he walked out on me and mom. Not a birthday card or even an appearance at graduation. Nothing. I hadn't even seen his face until it appeared on the news. For two days, I'd thought he'd done it. So had everyone in Cutthroat, and the police. That had been bad enough. But then Lucas had called and told me what he'd done—falsely admitted to killing Erin. For some reason, that made it even worse.

"What about yours?" I asked, diverting, hard core. This wasn't going to last, but dwelling on dear old dad wasn't going to get her back in my bed.

She took a sip of her beer, set the glass down on a coaster. "My parents? They're not assholes."

I tipped my head and the corner of my mouth tipped up. "One out of the three of us isn't bad."

"I want to know why Lucas' parents don't hate you. I mean, with your dad and all," Hailey commented.

I glanced to Lucas, who shrugged. "I have no fucking idea. I figured they'd be after me with pitchforks or something after what my dad did, but no."

It made no sense. They'd always liked me, at least they didn't outwardly hate me like they did with Kit Lancaster. That had been obvious since high school, back when she'd been friends with Erin, before she and Lucas even dated. But with what my dad did,

MOUNTAIN DELIGHTS

I'd expected to be eviscerated when I'd shown up with Hailey.

But no. Mr. Mills had slapped me on the back instead of punching me in the face.

"I've given up figuring them out," Lucas added.

So had I.

"Your turn, sweetheart. Your parents aren't assholes, you say."

"Right. I followed in my mom's footsteps," she added. "Like I said earlier, she skied competitively. Dad's learned to remain calm through yoga or Tai Chi. He has to be with two female daredevils in the family."

I lifted my glass, imagining a man who probably had white hair and an ulcer. "To your dad."

She gave me a small smile. "They live in Jackson. That's where I grew up."

I knew the town just over the Montana border in Wyoming. Pretty spot. Epic skiing.

Her cell rang, the same ringtone as before. Her coach. She looked down at it as if it were going to bite her.

"Sweetheart, talk to the man," I ordered.

She frowned, then sighed. "Fine. Hey, Mark," she said when she answered it.

While the bar music wasn't too loud for her to take her call, we couldn't hear what he was saying. But watching Hailey's face was indication enough that it wasn't all rainbows and unicorns.

"I've been busy. Yes, I know I should be training." She rolled her eyes. "Yes, PT is well. One hundred ten degrees. No, they haven't benched me."

She picked up her beer, took a swig.

I looked to Lucas, leaned in. "What's up with that?" I murmured, tilting my head toward Hailey.

MOUNTAIN DELIGHTS

"Snow's coming. Her coach is itching for her to get back to training. I met him at the mud run. He's hard core."

"I got that, but why's she not excited about it?"

"The Springs, tomorrow?" she said. "I don't know. Look, Mark, I'm not sure if I'm—"

She looked down at the table, listened. "Fine. I need a week. Yes, a week."

She swiped the screen, set her cell on the table.

"Everything okay?" I asked.

"He wants me in the Springs at the training center tomorrow." She laughed. "As if that's going to happen."

"Don't you want to train? To get back out there?" From the film clips I'd seen of her, she was incredible. Yeah, she'd had a horrible accident, but it wasn't stopping her. Was she afraid? Had she lost her nerve?

She shrugged, grabbed an unused coaster and started fiddling with it. "I'm happy here with you and Lucas. I like the way you keep me occupied."

I liked it, too. I grabbed her hand, tossed the coaster onto the table. "Sweetheart, I've fucked you good and hard and your ass is probably still sore from my palm, but we only met this morning."

She stiffened at that and tried to tug her hand away. Her blush told me she was equally parts embarrassed and angry.

"Hang on, don't pull away," I added, ensuring she didn't think it was a one-time thing. Fuck, no. Lucas gave me a death glare. I sighed, knowing I had to stop being so fucking blunt. "I want you here. With us. Me. This has been hot as fuck. Fun. Don't doubt that for a sec-

MOUNTAIN DELIGHTS

ond. But if you have to go to the Springs, wherever the fuck that is, you should go. We'll be here waiting for you." I winked. "Dicks hard and ready for more."

That pulled a smile from her.

"Cy's being an asshole, like usual," Lucas said, leaning in and kissing the top of her head.

I wasn't being an asshole, I was being the responsible one. I was all for fucking her brains out twenty-four/seven, but I had a feeling she was going to need some kind of challenge out of her life, besides me pushing her boundaries.

If she'd won championships, her drive to win wasn't like the average person's. She couldn't be as successful as she was without a challenge, a goal to achieve, whether it be one race or an entire season. I wouldn't let her slack off when it was clear racing was

VANESSA VALE

her life. I wouldn't get in her way either.

Besides, I wasn't the greatest of catches. She'd have her fun with us, check off the threesome thing from her bucket list and move on. I'd just enjoy it —and her—while it lasted.

"I'm scheduled to take a group of vets out," Lucas said, then looked to Hailey. "Just overnight. No matter how much I want to be in bed with you... hell, to stay in bed with you twenty-four/seven, people are counting on me. While I'm gone, maybe Cy can say something that doesn't piss you off."

"I can think of ways to keep her busy," I offered. On her knees. On all fours. Spread out on my kitchen table.

She squirmed in the booth, and I couldn't help but grin.

"I've liked your inventiveness so far. I told Mark a week, so he's coming here so we can head to training together."

MOUNTAIN DELIGHTS

She glanced at me, lifted one shoulder in a vague shrug. "He's counting on me," she said. "But that's because if I retire, he has no paycheck. I don't want to ski for *him*, I want to ski for *me*."

Retire at... what, twenty-six? Twenty-seven? No wonder she was having a tough time. When most people were just getting settled into a career, hers had the chance of being over.

The waitress brought a huge bowl full of spicy wings, three plates and a pile of napkins. I wasn't rich like Lucas. I wasn't born with a silver spoon in my mouth or even in the kitchen drawer. My mom worked two fucking jobs to keep all of us fed and clothed after my father bailed. My grandparents had died first, then Mom when I was eighteen and I'd been left the ranch. I wasn't flush with cash, but I was land rich. Every acre was mine. I had prime property, solid water rights and acreage that backed up to the National Forest. I'd had offers for millions, but I refused them all. Always would. While the ranch took a shit ton of work, I also helped Lucas with his non-profit. Helped with some trips, especially ones that used my horses.

As for Hailey, I had to guess she had money. Champion ski racers had big sponsors and they had big pockets. Hell, she might even be on a box of Wheaties.

"Then do that. Ski for yourself, which is the reason I thought you did it. If that's not the case, fuck your coach. What's his name again?"

"Mark Bastion."

"Mark's problems are not your problems. He's a grown ass man. Go ski the shit out of a mountain if that's what you want."

She grinned then. "Ski the shit out of a mountain?"

"You know what I mean," I replied.

MOUNTAIN DELIGHTS

"Okay, well, no snow out there yet. I've got a week to meet up with Mark and get back to pre-season practice," she continued, picking up a carrot stick and dunking it in the blue cheese dressing. "Until then, I want to be with you and not think."

I grinned, picked up a wing. Not think? I could get her to forget her own fucking name. "That can be arranged. While Lucas is off on his backcountry trip, you and I can get to know each other. In bed and out. And I promise, sweetheart, I'll make you forget everything but my dick."

8

We spent the night at Lucas' house, mainly because it was closest to the bar. None of us were big drinkers, but a few of their friends had shown up—fortunately, no one had mentioned anything about Cy's dad or Erin—and we'd stayed pretty late. By the time we got through Lucas' front door, they were all

MOUNTAIN DELIGHTS

over me, as if we hadn't had sex earlier at the ranch.

Twice.

Cy had woken early to return to the ranch for chores. While he'd said he had two people helping him with the cattle business and a few people who boarded their horses in his stable, he still had work to do. Animals needed tending no matter how sex weary one was.

Lucas and I hadn't slept much later, specifically because he was going on his overnight and wanted to get me off one more time before he left. A morning quickie.

A good way to wake up was with his head between my thighs, the rasp of his morning stubble brushing against my tender skin.

Of course, I'd reciprocated before getting dressed and driving him to the non-profit's office, a warehouse on the outskirts of town, to pick up the company van and stock the equipment needed for his trip.

I'd helped him for a bit, organizing sleeping bags, ensuring the water jugs were full. Before any of the men who were on the trip arrived, he'd kissed me one last time and sent me on my way, patting my ass as he did so.

And now I was headed toward Cy and his ranch, a smile on my face, and an ache in my pussy.

One thing I hadn't considered when agreeing to a fun threesome was how my body would be sore in ways and places I never imagined. Muscles ached, my pussy was a little tender from their very big dicks. Cy wasn't gentle, and that was A-OK by me. He was crazy bossy. No, he was a dominant. I doubted he'd ever been to a sex club or was into BDSM or anything, but he definitely had wanted me to submit. He'd

MOUNTAIN DELIGHTS

given me every opportunity to say no, but there hadn't been, for one second, a moment where I would have.

I wanted to be dominated. I wanted him to tell me what to do. I wanted him to spank my ass for being bratty. I wanted his dirty words, his dirty actions.

I wanted to submit. To give him my power. My accident had taken it away from me and I was lost. Out of control. The rush I got from winning a race, flying down the mountain at ridiculous speeds was like an orgasm. *Like* one. The absolute thrill. The intensity, the focused mind. Everything disappeared but the hill and me and my skis.

But then I wiped out. And that craving for control was gone.

And giving it to Cy obviously wasn't *keeping* control. I *gave* it to him. But that had been my choice. I'd wanted him to take over, to lead, to tell me what to do because I didn't know anymore. And besides the orgasms... god, they'd been incredible, he and Lucas made me whole again.

Crazy? Absolutely. I didn't completely understand it myself, but I craved more from Cy. It wasn't a downhill race, but it might just be better. Was it stupid to keep this going? Definitely. I was only going to get hurt, at least my heart. The fact that I was eager to get to him was a bad sign. This was turning into more than just *fun*.

A song I liked came on the radio and I turned it up, sang along. I was in the middle of nowhere on a two-lane road, the grasses a golden yellow from the cold weather. A dusting of snow blanketed everything, a reminder to me that my time was up.

I couldn't ignore the winter. I couldn't ignore the approaching race

MOUNTAIN DELIGHTS

season any longer. Mark had been right. It was time to get back into it.

But why did I not have the same excitement I usually did? The anticipation? Why did the idea of packing a bag and getting my passport filled with foreign stamps make me... depressed?

I loved Cutthroat. It was just like any other ski town in Montana or the Rocky Mountains. I'd been all over the world, been to towns just like it. But it called to me.

I put on my blinker—even though there was no one around—and turned on to the county road. No, Cutthroat didn't call to me. Lucas did. Cy now, too. Just the day before I'd taken this same drive not having met Lucas' best friend. And now I knew him intimately.

There wasn't just chemistry, but a connection. Was I driving to the ranch for that or for the really big dick and the guy who knew how to use it?

The radio went silent and I stared at it, confused. Then the dials on my dashboard dropped to zero. No speedometer reading, no oil temperature gauge. I stared, confused, then the car died. It didn't sputter, just cut out and I rolled, quickly slowing down without any power.

I glanced in my rearview mirror out of instinct, then steered the old SUV over to the side of the road where it rolled to a stop.

"Great," I muttered. The Land Cruiser had been my mom's when she'd been on the race circuit. She'd driven me to all my junior races in it, and when she'd bought a new car, I'd claimed it instead of her trading it in.

I loved the SUV—although it was made well before the term sport utility vehicle was ever coined, hell, before I was born—but it was moments like this

MOUNTAIN DELIGHTS

when I wished for something brand new.

Grabbing my bag off the passenger seat, I dug out my cell to call Cy. I paused, remembering I never got his phone number. I had no way to reach him. Lucas had his group of vets with him now, even if they hadn't headed off on their overnight. I couldn't call him.

Fortunately, there was cell service, and I looked up a tow company in Cutthroat... the *only* one in town. I sat playing a game on my phone as I waited the thirty minutes for the tow truck to arrive.

"Looks like you've got a bad alternator," the guy said, letting the hood drop back in place and wiping his hand on a rag he'd pulled from his jeans pocket after he'd taken a look to see what might be wrong.

I was leaning against the driver's door, staying out of his way.

"I'm not really sure what that means," I replied.

"An alternator helps charge the battery."

"So the car won't run because no power is getting to the battery if the alternator is bad."

He grinned, nodded. "You got it."

The man had introduced himself as Mac. If I weren't head over heels for Lucas and Cy, this guy could give them serious competition.

He should have been on the back of a Harley, not driving a tow truck. I was bundled up in a heavy sweater against the cool weather while he had on a black T-shirt with his towing company's button up thrown over top. A serious five o'clock shadow didn't hide his square jaw or full lips. And his gaze... penetrating, like he could see all the way to your soul. Yeah, he was that hot.

MOUNTAIN DELIGHTS

To top it all off, his right arm was covered in tattoos. A full sleeve.

Bad boy to the extreme, except he seemed pretty darn nice.

"I'm Hailey, by the way. Hailey Taylor."

He shook my hand and eyed me. "Lucas Mills' girl?"

I should have been offended at being called a girl, but he said it like Lucas and Cy did, in a possessive sort of way. I guessed we were together, it wasn't like any of us were with anyone else. I'd been classifying our... togetherness as *fun.* I was kidding myself because it was soooo much more, but admitting it aloud was dangerous. Even thinking of it kind of freaked me out. Still, it made it true.

Lucas and I weren't keeping our fling a secret, but we hadn't taken out a billboard or anything either.

"That's me."

"He's a good guy." He tucked the rag away. "Let's get it loaded up and we'll get you back to town. He wouldn't want you out here like this." He walked past me to climb in the tow truck and backed it up so it was right in front of my Land Cruiser.

"Actually, Lucas is off on a camping trip."

His dark eyes met mine. "Where were you headed then? Not much out this way."

"Flying Z ranch."

"Cy Seaborn's place?"

I nodded. I was all for being with Cy and Lucas, but after Lucas' parents' reaction to us being together, I was a little wary of sharing.

"You call him?"

I looked down at the road, kicked a pebble. "I don't know his number."

He glanced west as if he could see Cy's ranch, then back at me. "I know

MOUNTAIN DELIGHTS

him. He went to school with my younger brother. I'll dig up his number, and you can call him. If that doesn't work, I can drive you out to the ranch."

A cool breeze kicked up and I tucked my hair back.

He lifted his chin. "Climb into the rig. It's cold out here. Besides, I can't have you out here when I load up. Insurance issues."

I wasn't going to argue, happy to get warm.

AN HOUR LATER, Cy burst through the door of the repair shop. His eyes raked over the space until they landed on me. He sighed and his entire body went from rigid to relaxed. I went over to him, and he grabbed me and pulled me into his arms, into a hug that was a little too tight. He seemed to be comforting

VANESSA VALE

himself, not me, so I didn't say anything. Besides, I could feel the beat of
his heart against my ear, breathed in his
open air and clean male scent.

"You scared the shit out of me," he
murmured, then kissed the top of my
head.

I tried to step back, but he only loos-
ened his hold. I had to tilt my chin back
to look at him. His dark eyes roved over
my face as if to look for any injuries.

"Are you okay?"

I was surprised by his concern. I
hadn't driven off a cliff and the mechanic shop wasn't the ER. My alternator had died.

"I'm fine. Mac has been great."

Cy looked over my shoulder. "Good
to see you, Mac," he said, tucking me
into his side so I faced the mechanic.

A blatant display of possession if I'd
ever seen one.

Mac came over, shook Cy's hand.

MOUNTAIN DELIGHTS

"Been a long time. Shit deal about your dad."

I felt Cy tense and panicked at how he was going to respond.

All he did was lift his chin and say, "Yeah, shit deal."

Mac had said his brother had gone to high school with Cy, so maybe Mac knew the score with Dennis Seaborn. He'd probably said the right thing, acknowledged the elephant in the room, mentioned it as a fact and nothing more.

"Thanks for taking care of my girl," Cy said, moving the conversation away from his dad.

There was the *girl* thing again, but spoken in Cy's raspy growl of possessiveness, it was dang hot. Even though it shouldn't be true. I didn't belong to either one of them.

It was just *fun*.

Right?

He frowned, then looked to me. "I thought you were with Lucas Mills."

"She is," Cy explained.

Mac paused, glanced between the two of us, the way Cy was holding me in a blatantly possessive way. "Both of you? Totally works for me." He grinned, then nodded, as if that was that. "I've got to order the alternator, so it will be a few days. I've got your number when I have an update."

"Thanks," I replied, not sure what else to say. Mac didn't require more of an explanation, and if he did, what would I say? It was fun fucking two guys at once? I loved getting double the dick?

He and Cy said their goodbyes, and Mac went out into the service bay, leaving us alone in the waiting area.

Cy leaned down, set his hands on my shoulders so we were eye level. "I'm so fucking sorry, sweetheart."

MOUNTAIN DELIGHTS

I frowned at him, confused. "For what? It wasn't your fault my car broke down."

"Good thing you've got Lucas, too, because I was a dipshit. I didn't even think to give you my number. You were out there alone... *fuck.*" He leaned forward, setting his forehead to mine. "There is a killer on the loose," he snapped, but the tone didn't faze me. He wasn't mad at me. He was mad at himself.

I hadn't thought of that. I should have, because of Lucas. *And* Cy. God, it should have been in the front of my mind all the time. Hell, I'd gotten in a tow truck with a stranger who could be a murderer. Anyone in town could have done it, and I hadn't even thought about my safety for one second. But Cy had. Lucas, too, by ensuring Cy was with me while he was gone.

"Hey," I murmured. When he didn't

meet my gaze, I set my hands on his forearms. "Cy, I'm okay. I wasn't out there long."

"You shouldn't have been stuck out there at all. It's my job to keep you safe, and I didn't do it."

He meant what he said. Deep down. Like... a core belief of his that it was now his job to protect me. God, was it because of his dad, how he'd ditched his mom? Something broke for him inside me. I longed to take away his hurt.

"I wasn't there for you."

"You're here now," I said. "The second you heard, you came."

He nodded, rubbing the pad of his thumb back and forth over my lower lip.

Grabbing his face, I pulled him in for a kiss. Screw the thumb brush thing. It was gentle at first, soothing him and proving that I was fine. Then it turned fierce, because I wanted to

MOUNTAIN DELIGHTS

show him how much I appreciated his concern, but also so he knew I was fine. That I was in front of him, kissing him. I felt instantly at ease knowing he was there for me, that it seemed, he always would be. I felt I could trust him, and not just with my body. I couldn't avoid it any longer. My heart *was* involved now, too. That quickly, just one day, and I was in love with two men.

Shit. How was I going to leave them? How would I survive when they were done with me?

A door opened behind me and a throat cleared. I pulled back, blushed furiously.

Mac grinned at us, a mix of sheepish and sly at catching us. "Sorry, needed to get some paperwork."

He grabbed it off the counter and left us alone once again.

We'd been caught. God, tongues had

VANESSA VALE

been involved and lots of groping, Cy's hand was *still* on my ass.

I licked my lips. I tried to catch my breath, but all I wanted to do was climb him like a tree. We'd just been blatantly reminded we were in an auto shop, not his bedroom.

"You're blushing," Cy murmured. He didn't seem the least bit bothered by being caught out. We weren't sixteen, but still... "You've got two men fucking you and you're a little embarrassed by Mac seeing us together?"

I frowned. "It doesn't bother you that Mac saw us?"

"Me, kissing you? Fine." He spanked my ass, not hard, but a reminder. "He knows you're off limits. But naked? Hell, no. Hearing you come? Hell, no. I have to admit my inner caveman liked showing you off."

I had to admit I wanted him to grab

MOUNTAIN DELIGHTS

me by the hair and drag me back to his cave.

"Let's get out of here," he said, reaching down for my hand and leading me out to his truck. "I have plans for you. Without Mac watching."

Worked for me.

9

"This feels so good," she moaned.

Fuck, that kind of sound, and those words, should have been because I was balls deep inside her. But no, I wasn't even touching her. She was naked and she was turning me the fuck on.

"I figured you might be a little sore," I replied, climbing into the hot tub and settling next to her. It was dark and I

MOUNTAIN DELIGHTS

had no outdoor lights on, only the light of the moon brightened my back deck.

I'd driven her back to the ranch and suggested a dip in the spa I'd put in two years earlier. It was off the back deck with nothing but the prairie beyond. No other houses were around for miles. The sky was pitch black without any light pollution and the stars were a spray of light. I hadn't shared it with anyone, until now.

She opened her eyes and gave me a satisfied smile. Fuck, I loved having a wet, sexy, naked woman in here with me. Specifically, *Hailey*. Her hair, pulled up in a sloppy bun, curled from the humidity. Her cheeks were flushed and her tits bobbed along the surface. I was hard just looking at her. And that kiss earlier... I'd been good and restrained myself. I wasn't kidding about her possibly being sore. Neither Lucas nor I had small dicks. We had plenty to keep

Hailey satisfied, but until she got used to it, no doubt she needed a little break.

A *little* one, because the second she said she was good to go, I'd be right back in her. Her pussy was my new favorite place.

"I am," she admitted. "When I imagined being with two men, I didn't consider how voracious you'd be."

"Us?" I asked, settling my arms along the side of the tub. "You've come the most out of all of us."

She didn't reply, just closed her eyes again and settled into the hot water. I just looked at her. Even in the moonlight, I saw the freckles on her nose, the little scar by her eyebrow, her full lips.

I ran my hand over the back of my neck, remembering the way they'd stretched wide around my cock. I wasn't fucking her in the hot tub. It was way too hot. My dick didn't agree, but he wasn't in charge.

MOUNTAIN DELIGHTS

Neither was Hailey.

"Did you always want two men?" I asked.

She didn't open her eyes when she answered, but the water stirred when she lifted a shoulder. "I love reading romance books with two heroes. I guess that was a sign, getting hot for the books I read. I never imagined that happening to me in real life. Until Lucas."

"He just outright said he wanted to share you with me?"

Now she looked my way. Those blue eyes were soft, relaxed. Good.

"Lucas is a little kinky," she said. "So am I. We found that out pretty fast, our fucking getting wilder each time."

"Go on," I prodded when she got quiet.

"One time, he fucked me and played with my ass at the same time."

My dick was so hard right now, it was almost impossible not to lift her onto the edge of the hot tub, part her thighs and sink into her.

But no. Instead, I asked, "What, he finger fucked that tight hole?"

She nodded. A tendril of hair slipped from her bun and the end floated on the water. "He asked if I ever thought about having two cocks in me at the same time. I couldn't hide my interest in his question."

"You mean you got wet all over him."

"Oh yeah. After, well, we talked about it. I admitted the idea made me really hot. He'd said if I wanted, he'd share me with his best friend."

"Me."

She slid across the hot tub's bench seat to be closer. "You know the rest."

"Did Lucas know you needed to submit?"

She looked down into the water. Clearly, this was something new for her. I'd brought out a kink she may not

MOUNTAIN DELIGHTS

have known she had, or perhaps thought about but had never done.

"Look at me, sweetheart."

Her eyes met mine.

"Lucas will fuck you good and hard, but he won't be able to dominate you like I can. He won't get you on your knees at the door waiting for him when he comes home from a trip. He won't get your ass lit up in punishment, or even for the hell of it. He's just too damned nice."

When she opened her mouth to reply, I cut her off. "That's why he wanted me in the mix, because I can give you what he can't. I can give you what you've been missing, what you need."

I was learning pretty quickly what that was and it filled something in me, too. While she beautifully handed over her power to me, I took it as a gift. I dominated her only because she chose to submit, and it was a beautiful thing. I

VANESSA VALE

needed that control, that power exchange, because when my life was spinning out of control, it was one thing I could count on. I could be there for Hailey, give her what she needed even when she might not realize she needed something. For as long as she'd be around.

She turned so she was on her knees facing me. Her breasts came out of the water, dripping with water. The nipples were soft, plump tips from the heat.

I groaned.

"I need right now," she said, her voice breathy and like a fucking porn star.

"You're not sore?"

Biting her lip, she shook her head. "I... I ache."

Oh shit.

"You have a greedy pussy, don't you?"

"Oh yes," she quickly agreed.

MOUNTAIN DELIGHTS

"Who's in charge of that pussy, sweetheart? Do you decide when it gets fucked?"

When she shook her head, the tendril of hair clung to her long neck. "No."

"No, what?" I asked, making my voice have that edge of stern authority so she knew we were playing.

She blinked, wet her lips, then said, "No, sir."

Oh fuck. Why did that sound so damned good?"

"Yet you're so desperate for my dick that you'll beg anyway."

This was all foreplay. Talking dirty with her, starting things off so she knew I wasn't going to be gentle with her. I wasn't Lucas. Right now, she didn't want him. She wanted me.

"Please," she whispered.

I looked her over, took in the hooded eyes, the flushed cheeks, the wild hair. Her fucking luscious nipples. I almost gave in. But then I'd get what I wanted and not what she needed.

Hailey came first. Always.

"All right. You'll get me inside you, but *after* your spanking. Naughty girls who beg get fucked with a red, sore ass. Go to my bedroom and lean over the bed, feet on the floor."

She looked at me for a moment, then stood, the water sluicing down her toned, firm body.

Fuck, I could come from just looking at her. Now I had to spank her ass before I took her. My dick would have to deal.

Climbing out, she took two steps, then screamed.

Panicked, I stood up in the tub, looked for what freaked her out. My rifle was by the front door, dammit. I had a second to process the possibilities. She stepped on a nail. She kicked a

MOUNTAIN DELIGHTS

loose deck board and hurt her foot. Someone was in the house.

It was none of that.

It was a fucking skunk, just off the deck and in the grass. Less than ten feet from Hailey. I was only a few feet farther away.

"A skunk!" she said, freaking out, backing up slowly, as if seeing a bear or something fierce.

The black and white bugger was just as surprised to see us as we were to see him. I'd never seen one this close to the house before, but Jesus, this was bad. In a way, I'd rather see a bear.

I hopped out of the tub and pulled her into me. "Quiet, we don't want to get—"

The sentence wasn't finished before the skunk sprayed. Hailey screamed, I shouted and we both ran away from the animal. It was too late.

We were both swearing, gasping.

When I was a kid, one of my grandparents' dogs got sprayed by a skunk, a direct hit. We weren't covered, but the smell, fuck. It was in my nostrils, in my mouth. I watched as the skunk ran off, but the damage was done.

Holy. Fuck.

"Don't go inside!" I shouted, not wanting Hailey to take the stench into the house.

"Cy, we're naked and wet and we smeeeeeelllll!" she screeched.

At least we'd been in the hot tub long enough so we weren't cold. But we soon would be.

"Come with me," I said, taking her hand again and trying not to gag at the stench of us, hoping she really wouldn't puke, because if she did, I would. I led her around the house—away from the skunk—and to the garage, which wasn't attached to the house. I opened the side door, which was never locked, and went

MOUNTAIN DELIGHTS

inside. I found a clean horse blanket and gave it to Hailey.

"Okay, we need to go inside and at least get a phone so we can look up what to use to get rid of the smell."

She nodded, wild-eyed. Any thoughts of fucking were long gone. From now on, if I needed to will a hard-on away, I'd think of a skunk.

"We might puke, but we'll get through this. Together."

With her wrapped in a blanket—one that I'd be sure to throw out once we started getting cleaned up—we headed to the laundry room door. Thank fuck, my grandmother had been smart enough to put an outside entry into the room so that after a long day working the land, my grandfather wouldn't have to traipse through the house all muddy and smelling like cows with his dirty clothes.

I dashed into the kitchen, grabbed

my phone and returned, shutting the door to the laundry room behind me to keep our stench in, then did a search as Hailey tried to scrub her hands and arms with the soap at the utility sink.

"It says to use hydrogen peroxide, baking soda and dish soap," I said, reading the small screen. "I've got all that. Thank fuck."

Hailey looked up at me. Miserable. We smelled so fucking bad. "I'm never going outside again," she moaned.

As I looked in the under-sink cabinet for the hydrogen peroxide, I had to agree with her. This was not how I'd imagined the two of us getting to know each other. I'd wanted her naked and wet, but not like this.

LUCAS

. . .

MOUNTAIN DELIGHTS

I PULLED up in front of Cy's house, weary as hell. I smelled, needed a shave and eight hours of sleep in an actual bed. One that had Hailey in it. Naked would be preferable.

But I didn't see her old SUV. She'd been living with me while being in Cutthroat, and I'd driven by my place first. I'd assumed she'd be here with Cy, but I wasn't driving back to town now. I'd crash in one of the empty bedrooms here at the ranch.

The group I'd led had been up at dawn to hike out, and by the time everyone had left the warehouse, a successful trip done, it was after ten. Maybe Cy and Hailey had gone out for breakfast, but I couldn't imagine Cy letting Hailey drive her SUV. As if.

I went inside, paused. All was quiet. I went down the hall to Cy's room to see if they were sleeping in, but the bed was empty. Where the hell were they?

VANESSA VALE

The kitchen window over the sink was open, even though the morning air still had a sharp bite to it. The faint scent of skunk lingered, so I had to wonder if they'd opened it in the middle of the night to get fresh air and forgot about it.

Whatever. I went to the window, closed it.

I trudged to the bathroom Cy used on the main floor, stripped and took a Navy shower, soaped, rinsed and out in two minutes, too tired to stay in longer, even though the hot water felt fabulous.

I grabbed clean boxers from my bag and went upstairs to one of the empty bedrooms. I stopped in my tracks just inside the doorway. Cy and Hailey were in the bed, out cold, the sheets a tangle about them. Hailey's hair was a wild snarl around her head and she wore one of Cy's t-shirts. Cy was in boxers.

MOUNTAIN DELIGHTS

Why were they up here and not in Cy's room?

If they were sleeping this late, I had to wonder what they did all night. My dick hardened and tented my boxers. Cy had done Hailey, I knew that. How many times though to make them this worn out was the question. Had they broken his bed?

Lucky fucker.

I stepped up to the bed, tapped Cy on the foot. When he didn't stir, I did it harder.

He snorted, then turned his head to look at me. "Dude," he groaned.

"Wild night?"

He sniffed, scratched his balls through his boxers, then turned on his side to face Hailey. "You have no idea."

"Yeah, I have some idea," I countered, thinking of all the things they could do together.

He pushed up on his elbow, rubbed his eyes. "No, you have no fucking idea."

Hailey woke, then sat bolt upright. She blinked, looked around. Her hair stood out every which way. "I still smell it."

I frowned. "What, the skunk? I smelled it downstairs. The critter's long gone now."

Hailey turned her head, looked to Cy, clearly not amused, still half-asleep. "I think my nose is broken."

"Yeah. I know, sweetheart," Cy murmured, his voice taking on a quality I hadn't heard before. Somewhat... cherishing?

"Lucas, do we smell?" she asked.

"If you're wondering if I can smell sex all over you two, no."

"Get your head out of the fucking gutter, asshole," Cy said. "Do we smell like skunk?"

This was a weird-ass conversation.

MOUNTAIN DELIGHTS

"Why would you smell like skunk?"

"Because we got sprayed last night!" Hailey yelled. "Naked."

She burst into tears, Cy pulling her into his arms to hold her as she cried. Jesus, I'd never seen her like this before. Hell, I'd never seen Cy comfort a woman before either.

I just stared at them, wide-eyed. "You got sprayed by a skunk?"

"Naked," she repeated on a wail.

Cy wasn't rolling his eyes or challenging the words, only pulled her in closer, stroked up and down her back.

"Holy shit," I murmured. How had they been sprayed by a skunk... without clothes?

"I'm so fucking tired," he muttered. "Dude, we were up all night getting the scent off us. We came up here so we don't get the smell into my room, on my bed. This bed we can burn if we have to."

"I think I'm going to have a bald spot," Hailey said into Cy's bare chest, lifting her hand to her head.

Her hair was all there, but I wasn't sure if it would be after she tried to brush it. The only thing I'd heard to get rid of skunk smell was tomato juice... or ketchup.

"All night. Scrubbing with a mixture of shit in places that shouldn't have any kind of scrubbing."

"You put ketchup on your crotch?"

Cy glared at me. Seriously, we'd gone through some serious shit together and this was the look that should have killed me.

"What the fuck are you talking about? Hydrogen peroxide, baking soda and dish soap. It's like rubbing a bubbling, abrasive paste into your skin. I think my sense of smell is gone," Cy grumbled. "Please tell me we don't reek."

MOUNTAIN DELIGHTS

"You don't smell," I said honestly. There was a hint of skunk, but I never suspected they'd been sprayed.

Hailey lifted her head, looked to me with tear-filled eyes and a splotchy face. "Really?"

Cy gave me another look, one that said *don't fuck with her.* Clearly, they were exhausted and frazzled. What a nightmare. I had to hope we could all laugh about it. Later.

Now, it was time for all of us to crash. Hard.

"Really."

"How did this happen?"

"Two words," Cy said. "Hot tub."

Oh shit. Now I really wanted to laugh, but knew I'd be killed on the spot, and I had a feeling it would be a joint effort on their part.

"Move over and make room for me. I want to hold my girl."

I went to Hailey's side of the bed and

climbed in. Cy moved over to make room, and I pulled Hailey into my arms so I was wrapped around her. I sniffed as she rested her head on my bicep. "Nope, no skunk."

"That was awful and I'm so tired," she whispered, snuggling in. My dick liked it but now was not the time.

I looked to Cy who was staring at Hailey. He reached out, stroked her cheek and said, "Sleep, sweetheart. I'll be right here."

He dropped down onto his pillow, threw the blanket over all of us and closed his eyes.

They might not have had the night they wanted to get to know each other, but it seemed they had anyway. The way Cy had looked at her, the way Hailey just nodded in response and snuggled into me, they were tight now, tight in a way perhaps good sex couldn't have done.

10

I was cranky. It had been five days since the skunk incident and since then, I'd grown more and more restless. Irritable. Not because I smelled, because that had been resolved, thank God.

I could confront a mountain and ski the hell out of it, but I couldn't confront someone else. I *hated* confrontation. I didn't want to race anymore. I'd known that for months. I'd been kicking that can down the road, avoiding it, avoiding Mark.

I didn't want to say the words aloud to myself, let alone him. He was going to be pissed. Yell at me for throwing my career away. Wasting my talent. I was too young to give up. Besides my knee, I was healthy, and my knee had recovered enough to ski again. It could take the abuse; the doctors had said so. I probably wasn't even at the peak of my career. He saw more championship wins, more sponsorships, and he was probably right. More money for me, but more importantly, for him.

I was his meal ticket.

I never cared about the money. Fine, it was definitely a perk, but I had enough now. I didn't live lavishly. Hell, I drove a SUV that was older than me. I could walk away. Be a coach myself, get a gig as a commentator on a sports

MOUNTAIN DELIGHTS

channel for the sport. Work in the ski manufacturing industry. I had plenty of opportunities off the slope.

Or I could get back out there, ski the shit out of the hill, as Cy had put it. I'd wiped out before, recovered and got back on that lift. Did it all over again, faster and better.

What had changed?

Me.

I still craved that rush, that desperate need to control the mountain, my skis, even me. I was also scared. Scared to fall. To fail. To get hurt even worse.

I had Lucas and Cy. I loved what we had together, what we could become if given time, and that scared the hell out of me. I wanted to give up my racing career for two men.

It went against every feminist bone in my body.

Racing again would take me away

from them, from the life we were slowly building. It hadn't even been a week, but I didn't want it to stop. But it could be yanked away just as quickly as I'd fallen on that rough turn. I was putting my heart in the hands of two men, and they had the ability to crush it. I shouldn't want them. I should be back in the Springs, working my ass off.

I should be at training camp, then I'd jet off to the first race and never look back, not getting back to Cutthroat until the snow melted. April, if I was lucky.

April. Ugh.

But even knowing what Lucas and Cy could do to me, I wanted to quit. I was done. I'd lost the edge. The focus.

I had to meet with Mark to tell him. I dreaded it. He was intense, which was good as a coach. I needed his intensity, his drive. It matched mine, perhaps even more so. I didn't mind all that

MOUNTAIN DELIGHTS

aimed at me before a race, but now? It wasn't going to be pretty. He'd hate me.

"I thought you were going to wash the dishes?" Cy asked, coming in the kitchen door. He had three grocery bags in his hands, Lucas following carrying a few more. They sat them on the counter. I'd remained behind on the ranch when they went on a food run.

"Sorry," I said, joining them. "I forgot."

Cy gave me a look, one that said he wasn't pleased. Trying to get skunk smell off had bonded us. How was crazy, definitely, but we'd had a trauma, albeit a ridiculous one, and we'd survived together. He'd helped scrub my hair—over and over again—even though he'd reeked as well. He'd taken care of me, proven he'd be there for me in the worst of times.

It felt incredible, but that was dangerous. Everything that was exhilarating was also dangerous. I knew that first hand.

Since the skunk fiasco, he'd been sweet. Caring. Like Lucas. We'd had sex, countless times, but it had changed. It wasn't like the first days where he'd been bossy and dominant, spanking me and tying me up. When we'd been in the hot tub—and before the stupid skunk had ruined it all—Cy had ordered me into his bedroom to dominate me.

That had never happened, and not in the days since. No, he was sweet. Never talked dirty, never even spanked me. They never took me together, never mentioned fucking me at the same time like they had originally. They gave me orgasm after orgasm, but it wasn't enough.

I loved the attention, but it wasn't what I needed. God, what was wrong with me? Two men fucking me and I wasn't happy. Just as I'd thought, I was

MOUNTAIN DELIGHTS

destroying something before it even started. It was better this way. It was supposed to be fun. No heart involved.

I turned on the water on one side of the split sink, grabbed a dirty breakfast dish from the other side and rinsed it. Opening the dishwasher, I bent down to put it in, keeping my ass out. I had two virile men putting groceries away and they could have a show. I wasn't naked, but they could take the hint. Give me what I wanted. Just fun. Just... mindless sex.

Hopefully.

Rinsing another dish, I did it again. And again, wiggling my ass as I did so.

Lucas came up behind me, set his palm on my butt. "I like this."

Looking over my shoulder at him, I grinned. "It's yours for the taking."

What more invitation could I give him? I didn't want their kindness, their concern. I wanted their rough hands, their wildness.

He winked. "Let's go to Cy's room."

"No." Cy's voice was like a whip cracking. He leaned against the counter, arms crossed. "She doesn't get our dicks."

"What?" I sputtered. "Why not?"

"You've been a bad girl."

"Because I didn't do the dishes?" I asked, stunned.

"That, and the fact that you didn't call your parents back yesterday. Did you?"

My cheeks flamed, knowing he was right. They'd left a message, and I had yet to call them.

"No."

"Other things, too." He stroked his beard.

There *had* been other things. I'd left wet towels on the floor. Stupid shit that was ridiculous, just to get a rise out of

MOUNTAIN DELIGHTS

Cy. To get him to *do* something besides kiss me on the head and love me. Yeah, love. I didn't want the love.

I wanted the fun. The fucking. Nothing else. That was *fun.* Safe.

And so, I lashed out. Acted out so they'd have to give it to me. I grabbed another dish, rinsed it and put it in the dishwasher with the others.

"Sweetheart, if you wanted a spanking, all you had to do was say it."

My head whipped up, met his dark gaze. "What?"

"You need to be taken in hand, don't you?"

"I—"

"We'll give you whatever you need, but being a brat won't work."

Shit, he was right. It hadn't worked. The towel thing had been petty and so like a moody teenager. Not doing the dishes had been for attention and I'd gotten it, but in the wrong way. He wasn't tossing me over his shoulder to drag me to his room for a wild time.

"Sorry," I muttered. I'd never behaved like this before. Petty. Shallow. Self-serving. Why couldn't I be satisfied with their affection? *Because you are afraid of it!*

"You will be."

And with those words, goose bumps rose on my arm, my pussy clenched. Those three words were what I'd wanted to hear all week.

He walked out of the kitchen and sat down on the edge of the coffee table. "Come here, sweetheart."

I glanced at Lucas, who only winked at me again. He was not going to offer me any help, wasn't going to hug me or kiss me or even fuck me. Knowing he would be watching whatever Cy intended made me all the hotter.

Slowly, I made my way over to Cy, and he set his hands on my hips, pulled

MOUNTAIN DELIGHTS

me in between his parted knees. His hold was gentle, but when he looked up at me, his gaze was as dark as his voice. "You need to be spanked, don't you?"

I bit my lip, nodded. I did. "You wouldn't give it to me."

One dark brow winged up. "So you acted out?"

"I'm sorry," I repeated.

"I'll give you whatever you need. Lucas, too. But not this way. Manipulating me. Trying to make me angry."

Oh god, that's what I had been doing. My frustration seeped away and was replaced by disappointment. In myself.

He took my chin between his fingers, and I had no choice but to look into his dark eyes. "I will *never* touch you if I'm mad, so your little plan didn't work."

"You've been too nice," I said, blinking back tears. "I don't want nice."

VANESSA VALE

He laughed. "Most women want that."

I frowned. "I'm *not* most women."

His hands went to my jeans, undid the button and slid down the zipper. "Yes, Lucas and I are well aware you are one of a kind."

"We're fucking lucky that you're ours," Lucas said, dropping down onto the couch, watching as Cy pushed my jeans and panties down around my thighs.

"I wanted what you promised in the hot tub."

Cy paused, thought about our pre-skunk conversation.

"Over my lap," he ordered.

I paused and he waited. This was what I'd wanted for days. What I'd craved. I'd never been spanked before meeting Cy, and it had been a revelation.

I turned and settled myself over his

MOUNTAIN DELIGHTS

strong thighs, my palms pressing into the floor. His hand settled on my up-turned ass, stroked over it.

"This is a pretty sight. Let's make it prettier. Lucas, go get that plug and lube I picked up."

My bottom clenched at Cy's words.

"The medium sized one."

Oh god.

From my position, I saw Lucas' feet as he walked past. When had Cy bought a butt plug? I didn't even know there was an adult store in town.

"Now, let's get you warmed up for that plug."

Cy's hand came down on my ass and I jumped. It wasn't all that hard, and I'd been expecting it, but still…

He spanked me again, the other side. Then again. And again. Each time, his hand fell a little bit harder. By the time Lucas returned, my bottom was all warmed up and it tingled.

My core ached, my pussy throbbed with need. *This* was what I'd missed. My mind instantly cleared. My problems were washed away every time his hand landed on my ass.

I wasn't in control. Cy was. The sting reminded me of that. It settled me.

His fingers tugged on one cheek, opened me up, and I gasped when a drizzle of cool lube landed directly on my back entrance. Immediately after, I felt the hard pressure of the plug working its way in.

"Relax," Cy said, adding more pressure.

"Easy for you to say," I grumbled. "You don't have something going into your ass."

A hand came down on my ass. Hard. Then again.

"Do you want the big plug instead?"

I shook my head, my hair falling

MOUNTAIN DELIGHTS

around me like a curtain. That plug wasn't big? "No."

"No, what?" he asked, spanking me again.

"No, sir."

He rubbed my sore flesh as he pulled back on the plug, then pressed once again. I took a deep breath, let it out. Relaxed. All at once, the wide flange opened me up and the plug sank deep. It didn't hurt, not any more than Lucas' fingers had, but this was different. It was ungiving and it wasn't going anywhere.

"Look how pretty that ass is," Cy commented.

"Gorgeous," Lucas agreed. His voice came from the couch, but I hadn't paid any attention to the fact that he'd sat back down.

"Time for your spanking, sweetheart."

I tensed. "It hasn't started?"

"Oh, no, that was just a warmup. When you're naughty, you get punished inside and out."

"Oh god," I moaned. I loved his dirty talk and the way my pussy was on full display, he no doubt could see it. I was wet. Ridiculously wet, and all because he was in charge.

His hand came down again, and I gasped, tears burning my eyes. His fingers had bumped the flange of the plug, and it shifted inside me.

"Ow!" I cried, reaching back instinctively to cover my ass.

He took my wrist, held it pinned behind my back as he spanked me again. And again.

By the third one, I was crying. I lost count after that, letting it all out. The heat and sting were intense, but this was what I'd wanted. What I'd craved for days. What I'd been bratty to get.

I gave up. Gave over. I melted over

MOUNTAIN DELIGHTS

his thighs, letting him spank me. As soon as I did so, he stopped, then carefully lifted me up into his lap, my jeans and panties still tugged down, the plug still firmly in my bottom. He held me as I cried, as I just let go.

"I'm sorry," I muttered into his chest. "I'm not a crier."

He stroked my hair. "Maybe you should be. You're too strong, sweetheart. We're here for you, good and bad."

They were, but I didn't want that. I wanted them to fuck me now, especially with the plug in my ass at the same time. God, it would be so tight.

"What's eating at you?" Lucas asked.

I tipped up my chin, looked at him. He was leaning forward, elbows on his knees.

"You can tell us now, sweetheart, or after I spank your ass some more," Cy added.

"I don't want to race anymore."

I said it aloud. I said the words I'd been thinking for months.

Lucas grinned. "That wasn't so hard, was it?"

I nodded. "God, yes, that was *really* hard."

"Why don't you want to compete?" Cy asked.

"I'm done. I've... lost my nerve, I think. Or at least the drive."

"That's why you want me to spank you? To fill that void?" Cy shifted me in his lap. "You have control on the mountain. Complete control of the turns, the skis, the fucking mountain. Then you fall and it takes that from you. You what, want to give it to me, now?"

I frowned. What he said made sense. Why did I want to give my control to him, though? I'd been fighting my interest in them all along. I didn't want to

MOUNTAIN DELIGHTS

want them more than for just a fun time.

I shouldn't have given it to him, but I wanted it. I needed it, it seemed.

Cy looked to Lucas.

"We want to be with you. Forever, doll," Lucas said. "But you have to find your thing; you have to live your life. We'll be beside you while you do it. If that's ski racing, great. If it's not, great. But you can't lay over Cy's lap to forget. You need to make yourself happy, whatever you decide."

"That's right," Cy added. "I'll spank your ass. Fuck it, and hopefully soon. But I won't dominate you as a replacement."

"So, you're saying you think I should ski?"

Lucas shook his head. "I'm not saying one way or the other. You have to decide what's right for you. Only for you. Quit for *you,* but don't replace skiing with us."

Was that what I'd been doing? Had I unintentionally been doing exactly what I'd tried to avoid?

"You can't hide here like you have been," Cy said.

"I'm not hiding!" I countered.

He just stared at me for a minute, then continued. "We won't enable that. If you don't want to compete anymore, that's fine. But you need to go talk to your coach. End it."

Wait a minute. Wait. A. Minute.

"You won't *enable* me?" I asked. "This week was supposed to be fun! To have sex with two hot guys. You weren't enabling me, you were *fucking* me."

Lucas perked up at that. "Fun? You think all we're having is fun?" He ran a hand over his neck, clearly thinking this was much more than that.

"Yes, enabled," Cy continued. Fuck,

MOUNTAIN DELIGHTS

he was like a dog with a bone. "You didn't connect with your parents, who, I would guess, want to know about how you're feeling, what your plans are. Same goes with your coach. He's been calling you all the time, wanting to know when you would get back to training. Even coming here to meet with you. You stalled him for a week to be with us. I'd say we enabled you."

Lucas scowled at me.

I sputtered, stunned by what he was saying. "What's wrong with wanting to be together, to have fun?" I countered. Hadn't they wanted to be with me? They'd certainly seemed content fucking me. "People do it all the time."

"To stall," Cy added.

"To fuck," I snapped, not liking this at all. He made it sound like I'd been using them.

"To stall," he repeated.

I stood then, pointed at him.

VANESSA VALE

"You're one to talk. You've been avoiding your dad just as much as I've been avoiding talking to Mark. You used this week the same way I did."

"She's got you there, asshole," Lucas muttered.

Cy tilted his head, ignored Lucas. "I haven't seen my dad since I was nine. This week didn't change anything."

"Oh? You've been hiding out in your house. You said so last week when I showed up. Avoiding town. The only way you're going to get resolution with your dad, to know why he claimed to have killed Erin, is to confront him. You've been hiding from the reporters, but really, you've been hiding from the truth. Your dad has more answers than just having to do with Erin's murder."

Cy circled his finger in the air around us. "This whole thing isn't about me."

MOUNTAIN DELIGHTS

"Yeah, I know. I'm the one with the plug in my ass."

God, I was standing there with my pants halfway down, my ass probably bright red, and a plug was shoved inside me. They could see my pussy, the way my thighs were still wet, although I was no longer the least bit aroused. Reaching back, I pulled out the plug. Carefully, slowly, and with a wince. It wasn't that great a feeling when I wasn't into it.

I dropped it to the floor then yanked up my panties and jeans.

"Yes, I did petty shit to get you to spank me. I seem to need it. The release. Like you said, I've lost control and you give it to me. Yes, it totally sounds weird. I just hadn't realized I'd been acting out because of my job. I see it now. And you're right, I do need to come to terms with what I'm going to be when I grow up."

I finished fumbling with the button, then stepped back. Pointed. "But you, talk about cranky. You're the king of avoidance. God, you pulled a rifle on me when I first showed up because you were pissed about your dad. So, don't get all righteous and bossy when you're the one who needs to get his shit together."

Lucas laughed, shook his head.

I went to the little table by the front door, grabbed Lucas' truck keys—my SUV was still at the mechanic's—and my bag, looked to him. "I'm taking your truck and going to your house. Alone."

"Doll, wait," he countered, standing up. "We need to talk about this. You need to know I feel like what we have is more than fun."

I loved Lucas, knew Cy's actions—or *inactions*—weren't his issue, but still. I didn't want to be hugged and coddled right now. I wanted to stew in my anger

MOUNTAIN DELIGHTS

for a little while. Drink some wine, fume. "This wasn't supposed to get heavy, Lucas. Fun. *Fun.* FUN. I wasn't trying to get my heart involved. Or yours. It hurts too much, to lose the things you want."

"Then don't push me away," he said, his pale eyes pleading. "You've got me. I'm right here. I'm all in. And so is Cy if he ever got his head out of his ass."

"I want to be alone, Lucas."

He studied me, then nodded. "All right. For now."

I exhaled, relieved he didn't push to come with me. I needed time to be angry.

"I'll handle Mark. My parents," I told him. Then, to Cy, I added, "Let me know when you deal with your dad. Until then, go stick that plug up your ass."

11

"Want me to come with you?" Lucas asked as he climbed from my truck and shut his door. He leaned back against it, crossed his arms.

It had snowed overnight, leaving a dusting of white over everything. My breath came out in a white cloud. Thick clouds hung low, dark like lead, just like

MOUNTAIN DELIGHTS

my mood. There would be more snow before the day was over.

I came around the front of the vehicle and faced him. "Hold my hand, too?"

Lucas slowly shook his head. "Asshole," he muttered.

I looked to my father's house, shut my eyes. The place had been built during the great depression. A small, squat box with wood siding. Two windows flanked the front door. Fifty years ago, it may have been blue, now it was an uneven gray with paint flaking away. The roof needed to be replaced, patched here and there as if the owner couldn't afford more than a quick repair job. The whole house sagged to the left. The lawn was non-existent, a mix of dirt and tall weeds. The concrete walkway from where we parked on the unpaved road to the front door was buckled and heaved. The farmland that surrounded the house hadn't been plowed in years, from the looks of it. I had to wonder if it was part of my father's parcel or if he only owned the small bit of yard along with the house. The nearest neighbor was a half a mile down the road.

The place was a fucking mess. It was unbelievable my father had walked away from me and my mom for this.

"You're here so I don't kill him. That's all," I reminded.

"And you're here because Hailey handed you your fucking ass."

The fucker was right. After Hailey had stormed out, I'd received a second telling off by Lucas. Not only had I pissed her off enough that she didn't want to see me, but she hadn't wanted to see *him* either. If she'd said the word *fun* one more time, I figured Lucas would have spanked her ass.

Had she really thought all we were doing was fooling around? Having a

MOUNTAIN DELIGHTS

good time? We'd been sprayed by a fucking skunk together! If that wasn't bonding, I had no idea what the fuck was. And now he was pissed at me. Watching me. Hell, he was babysitting me so I'd get this over with so we could get back to Hailey. He'd made it very clear he'd had to jerk off in the shower instead of getting inside our girl. I was officially a cock blocker and going to get more than a verbal beat down if I didn't get this over with.

As for Hailey, I was going to have to fucking grovel.

He'd stayed the night at the ranch, giving Hailey the room she'd wanted. He'd texted her, which had reassured him she was fine.

I glared at him now, but he wasn't fazed. This was my shit show, and he was only here for backup.

Hailey was right. I had to confront my dad. I had to know the truth. It was eating me up not knowing. There were seven billion people in the world, and just one was ruining my life.

I wanted Hailey in it. I wanted her over my lap. Under me. Any way I could get her. Turned out, Lucas and I were right for her. *I* was right for her. I gave her something she needed, something she only got from me. And in return, she gave me something. Love, although she'd probably throat punch me before admitting it, and her trust.

Her trust was like a drug I couldn't live without. And that was why I was manning the fuck up and dealing with my dad.

And the glare Lucas was sending my way.

"Fuck," I breathed, then made my way to the door.

It opened before I could knock.

My breath caught as I got my first

MOUNTAIN DELIGHTS

real glimpse of the man who'd made me since I was nine. There had been footage of him as he'd left the police station, his mug shot. I knew he'd aged, but now... he looked a decade older than fifty-five. I remembered his dark hair—something I got from him—but it was white now. Thinned. His face had deep creases as if he were a pack a day smoker. His eyes were droopy, his clothing too big for his frame. I also got his height, but his shoulders were stooped.

This was a shell of the man he once was.

"I heard you pull up."

Of course, he did. There was nothing else around. The sound of my truck couldn't be missed unless you were dead.

"Why did you do it?" I asked. I wanted answers and I wanted gone.

"Come in," he offered, stepping back.

All I could see of the interior was sparsely furnished. Old.

"No. I'll stay right here."

I didn't want in his house, in his life. I just wanted answers.

He gave a slight nod of understanding.

"Why did you do it?" I repeated.

He scratched his head, and I watched dandruff fall like snow onto his gray sweatshirt.

"Left your momma?"

There was so much I wanted to know, but it had been eighteen years. Too much time. Mom was gone now. What did it matter?

"Why did you say you killed Erin Mills?"

"I figured you wanted to know why I left you."

"Fine, tell me."

I felt silly standing on his front stoop. We probably looked silly, him

MOUNTAIN DELIGHTS

letting all the warm air out of his house.

"The mill closed. I lost my job. There was no work for me in Cutthroat anymore. I began to drink. To gamble. Let's just say I lost more than money."

I made a funny sound, like a laugh, but it wasn't funny. "All the shit Mom had to deal with all because of excuses that took you two seconds to say."

I wasn't sympathetic at all.

"It was complicated."

"It was life," I countered. "You had a wife, a child. You should've manned up. Got a job at the fucking Quickie Mart by the highway."

His dark eyes narrowed and my heart skipped a beat, recognizing the same gesture in myself. "I did. I manned up. I let you two go. I wasn't worth it."

"She worked two jobs. *Two.*"

He nodded. "I know."

"She worked herself to death." I

VANESSA VALE

pointed at him, let my arm drop. "And you… you're still alive."

His lips pursed, but said nothing.

"Why did you say you killed Erin Mills?"

"You asking or is Lucas?" He tipped his chin in Lucas' direction.

"Everyone in Montana's asking. I figure I have the right to know more than any of them."

"I manned up."

I stared at him, waiting for more. "What the fuck does that mean?"

He shrugged his bony shoulders.

"That's it? That's all you have to say?"

"That's it."

I took a step back, stared at the man. He was a stranger to me.

"You have nothing else to say?"

He blinked, then again. "Cyrus, you won't believe me, but I'm proud of you.

MOUNTAIN DELIGHTS

I've followed you, watched you turn into a man. A *good* man."

My heart ached. Not for the stranger in front of me, but for the father who had disappeared, who I'd hoped to have had. Who'd never existed.

"Because of Mom."

A tear slid down his weathered cheek and he wiped it away. "All because of her. You might look like me, but looks aren't everything. You've got her heart. Her soul." He cleared his throat. "Goodbye, Cyrus."

He shifted, then closed the door.

I stared at it, realizing I'd gotten jackshit out of him. I still had no idea why he'd claimed to have killed Erin. Glancing over my shoulder, I looked to Lucas. He hadn't moved. Should I bang on the door, force him to tell me? He was weak and pathetic. I'd beat the words out of him in seconds.

I'd gotten closure with the guy. He was nothing like I'd been hoping he'd be. Still thirty-seven years old and full of life and loving my mother, being a father to me. He hadn't been that man for a long time.

I mourned the loss of the father who had disappeared, but I didn't want who he'd become. My mom had been better off without him. Maybe he'd known that and stayed away.

I turned on my heel, walked back to my truck.

"Well?" Lucas asked.

I shook my head. "He wouldn't say."

I wasn't going to tell my best friend that my father had told me he'd falsely admitted to murdering his sister because he'd *manned up*. What the fuck did that mean?

"Don't you want to find out?" he asked.

I ran a hand over my beard, sighed.

MOUNTAIN DELIGHTS

"If you want, I'll kick the door in and make him talk."

Lucas looked toward the house. "I want to know. Fuck, I do. But this was about you. About closure or forgiveness or some shit like that."

I opened my truck door, my gaze looking past Lucas to the house. "There's nothing here. I lost him years ago."

I had. I just hadn't realized it. Dennis Seaborn had been dead to me since I was nine. I just hadn't buried him. Now I had.

"That's fucking closure right there."

12

Cy was right. I had to face my shit. And I'd been using him and Lucas as a way to delay the inevitable. And I'd been doing that with them, using them to put it off. When it changed from just a good time to something more, I had no idea. Maybe it was the first time I saw Lucas at the mud run. Maybe it was when Cy and I had been sprayed by that

MOUNTAIN DELIGHTS

asshole skunk. Maybe it had been building all along. I'd not only gotten exactly what I'd wanted, an amazing time with two men, I'd gotten exactly what I hadn't wanted.

Love. And that scared the shit out of me. Enough to drive them away. To run away. To avoid. Again.

Ever since I'd told them I wanted to quit, I hadn't changed my mind. Of course, it had only been overnight, but I knew it would stick. I'd still ski, that wasn't going to change, but I wasn't going to compete anymore.

I hadn't told them, but I'd lost my nerve. That accident had been brutal and to shave off the difference between winning and something like eighth place—which sometimes was less than a thousandth of a second—was to go all out.

I couldn't do that anymore. I didn't *want* to. Not if it risked so much.

I'd lucked out that I'd only needed knee surgery.

Even though I was decided, I wasn't thrilled to tell that to Mark. My parents had been easy when I'd called. They understood. Perhaps, they were content with me giving it up because I had wiped out so badly that it had shaken them, too.

They wanted me happy, but they also wanted me alive and in one piece.

Mark didn't have any skin in the game when it came to my career. At least not blood. I was his cash cow and he was driven not for me, but for himself.

If I quit, he lost his cut. He lost the recognition of being the champion's coach. The connection to the sponsors, to the big-league players in the racing world. I was his meal ticket.

It was time to live my life for myself, not for a dream that I'd had since I was

MOUNTAIN DELIGHTS

a kid, not because I wanted to be like my mom.

I wanted to be me. And if I were truly honest, I wanted to be with Cy and Lucas. For more than just fun.

As for a job, I had an idea. I wanted to lead some group trips for Lucas' non-profit. Ski trips. Whether they were just day outings to Cutthroat Mountain or winter camping trips where we cross country skied into the backcountry. Either way, it sounded ideal. Fun. Calm. And with people who could really use my help and guidance.

Maybe I'd even teach a few kids' classes at the resort because I remembered what it was like to first discover the thrill of racing down a mountain, even if it was the flattest of green runs.

I'd texted with Lucas. I wasn't mad at him, only afraid of what loving him meant. And, it wasn't his fault Cy was an asshole sometimes. I was amazed he'd given me space, allowed me to be pissed, to think. The downside of having two men in my life is that I didn't have a lot of time to myself. To stew. To drink more wine than I should have.

He knew I was meeting with Mark this afternoon, was okay that we'd meet at his house. I knew Mark would be angry, and I didn't need him to make a scene at a restaurant or any other public place.

When this was over, I'd go to the ranch. Talk it out with Cy. I didn't *hate* him. The opposite. I loved him. I really did. Crazy, definitely, but I was wired crazy.

We'd argue perpetually, definitely more than me and Lucas. But he was worth it. And if he never wanted to deal with his dad, I didn't blame him. Me avoiding Mark and him steering clear of the man who'd abandoned him as a

MOUNTAIN DELIGHTS

child, then fucked with Lucas' family, was something else entirely.

The doorbell rang and I smiled, resolute in my plan, eager to get back to the ranch and my men. To make it right with them. God, the makeup sex we'd have!

I was finally eager to talk with Mark, to get it over with, so I could move on with my life.

"Hey," I said, when I opened the door for my coach.

He lifted his chin in reply, came inside. I hadn't seen him since the mud run, the day I'd met Lucas. He looked the same, perhaps his tan had faded a bit.

He was in his usual uniform of track pants and a fleece pullover. He was in his thirties, attractive, although I'd never been into him. He'd raced for the Olympic team, although he'd never stood on a podium. Never got close to it.

"This where you're shacking up now?" he asked, looking around. For all of Lucas' family money, his place was pretty tame. An old miner's house from the early days of Cutthroat. He'd obviously updated it since then, but it was still a tiny two bedroom. No garage. No pool or solarium or any other fancy stuff his parents had in their house. He'd told me he lived off his earnings from the non-profit, not his trust fund.

"This is it," I replied. There was no reason to say more, to tell him it wasn't *shacking up.*

He clapped his hands together. "Okay, you've gotten some dick, now it's time to get your head back in the game."

I froze at his crude words. "Excuse me?"

He laughed and held his hand up. "I

MOUNTAIN DELIGHTS

understand. Believe me, I do. But you've had your fun. The way I see it, you can do Lillehammer as a warmup, then we'll be ready for Wengen by January."

God, when he said the word *fun,* it sounded so tawdry. Was that what Lucas and Cy thought when I'd tossed it at them?

"Mark, look," I began.

He held up his hand. "Don't say you're quitting."

"I'm quitting."

There, I'd done it. He could leave now, and I could go to the ranch and get some more of that dick that he says has been distracting me.

Perhaps it had, but it seemed I'd needed a little distracting, and needed it for the rest of my life.

"Are you fucking kidding me?" he shouted.

I stepped back at his sudden shift from his usual slightly aggressive tone

VANESSA VALE

to anger. His face turned red and a vein bulged at his temple. It only drew my eye to his receding hairline.

"No, I'm done. I'm sorry, Mark, but that accident finished me."

He looked to my leg, as if he could see my knee through my jeans. "You said you had almost full range of motion and that you're cleared."

"I am."

"Then let's go." He thumbed over his shoulder toward the door. "We can be in the Springs by morning."

I shook my head and stepped back again, bumped into the couch.

"I said no. I'm done. You can go to the Springs, but I'm not going with you."

His eyes narrowed and he advanced on me. "You uppity bitch. I'm your coach. You don't say when you're done. I do."

I should have been pissed at him like

MOUNTAIN DELIGHTS

I had been with Cy for bossing me around. With Cy, I wasn't scared. I wasn't afraid he'd hurt me. But Mark, now? I was angry at the way he was talking to me, but I was afraid of him more.

"Ever since you met that rich Mills kid, you've been off the rails."

I stepped to my right, moved away from the couch, away from Mark. "I've felt this way longer than I've known Lucas."

"Trust me, I know what it's like to fuck a Mills. Pretty sweet stuff. But the flavor doesn't last."

I stared at him. What? *What?* He'd fucked Lucas? What the hell was he talking about.

Then it came to me and I freaked. Holy shit. He wasn't talking about Lucas. He was talking about Erin. He'd fucked Erin Mills.

"You need to go now," I said, trying

to cut past him to get to the front door so he'd leave.

Instead, he grabbed my arm, shook me so my teeth snapped together.

"Oh, no. We're not done, Hailey. We're just getting started." He'd fucked her. Had she made him mad? Oh God, had he killed her?

The strike across my face made me see stars.

LUCAS

WE WERE at the diner eating a late lunch. I'd decimated my burger and was lazily picking at my fries. Not much was said on the ride back to town. Cy was lost in his thoughts. He'd talked to his dad for the first time in almost

MOUNTAIN DELIGHTS

twenty years. It was something to process.

"You're too fucking calm," he said, looking across the table at me. The waitress brought a refill on his iced tea and he thanked her.

We were at one of the booths in the back corner. I could see out into the parking lot, which was quickly emptying as it was the end of the lunch rush.

I glanced at him, shrugged. "What else can I do?" I tossed a fry in my mouth.

His dark gaze flared, not with heat, but anger. "Steal my truck and go back to my father's house, make him talk."

It was a tempting idea, one I'd considered more than once since we pulled away.

"He didn't kill Erin," I said. "The traffic camera photo of her blew his story wide open. She was alive when he'd said he killed her. While he did a shitty thing by stepping forward, it wasn't him. I'd rather focus my attention on finding who really did do it."

Slowly, he shook his head. "Jesus, just once I want to see you lose your shit and rip someone's head off."

I couldn't help but grin at the image. I was calm and he'd always hated it. In comparison, he was like a bull in a china shop. He had a hair trigger, and I had to admit, when we'd driven to see his dad, I'd expected to have to hide a body before we left. Maybe he realized, no matter how much he wanted to, his father wasn't worth the effort.

"I'm sure there will be a time."

My cell chimed and I lifted it from the table. "It's Nix."

Cy sat up straight. Hearing from the detective meant they knew something. I glanced at the screen.

MOUNTAIN DELIGHTS

"He wants to run some names by me."

That meant they hadn't caught Erin's killer. I wrote out a reply, letting him know where we were. I watched the bubbles on the screen as he typed out his response.

"He's coming here," I told Cy, setting the phone down and grabbing another fry.

"Heard from Hailey?"

I tried not to grin, but it was hard. "You sound like a seventh-grade girl."

He smiled. "I fucked up, and now I wonder if I've blown it for good."

"Doubtful. She's not shallow. A little arguing won't keep her away. She loves you. Me. *Us,* even if she hasn't said it yet."

"You think?"

I ached a brow. Total seventh-grade girl.

He sighed, realizing how he was be-

VANESSA VALE

having. It was reassuring to know he cared about her. I'd seen it all along and now he was blatantly whipped.

"I doubt it will be the last time we fight."

I laughed at that. "You two are always going to knock heads. Did you really want someone meek and quiet?"

He glanced out the window, thought. "Her submission's all the sweeter when she gives it to me."

My dick got hard remembering how she'd just let go for him. How that plug looked nestled between her perfect ass cheeks.

"She's meeting with her coach. We'll wait for her text when she's done, then go get our girl. Celebrate her decision."

"Did you want her to race?" he asked.

"The video of her accident..." I shuddered remembering it. "Fuck, I don't want that to happen again. But

MOUNTAIN DELIGHTS

then I look at videos of her other races, of her crossing the line first. The… exuberance and thrill on her face. She's amazing. I'll stand beside her whatever she wants to do, but I'd probably get a fucking ulcer if she got back out there."

He took a swig of his tea. "No shit." He pointed toward the parking lot. "Nix is here."

That was fast. We weren't too far from the police station, but they'd have needed their siren to get here that quick. I had to assume they'd been already in their SUV when he texted.

Nix walked toward the diner's entry with his partner, Miranski. I'd met her a few times before, the first right after Erin had been killed. She was tall and lean with long, dark hair. I'd call her pretty, but she was also serious, which was probably important for her job. I'd also say she was driven, just like Hailey, but in completely different ways. Mi-

VANESSA VALE

ranski was driven to see my sister's killer was behind bars, and I respected her for that.

She and Nix were good detectives, but they were on a hard case. Not only had there been no leads since it was discovered Cy's dad had been lying, but they had a lot of pressure from the media, the mayor and even my parents to find out who did it. Small towns and murderers on the loose weren't a good combo.

Standing in the entrance, they looked around, then found us. Miranski headed our way, but Nix stopped to say hi to Kit, his girlfriend, a waitress here. She was working the tables on the other side of the restaurant, but I could see him lean down and kiss her forehead. She said something to him and he smiled, then stroked her hair before working his way toward us.

I'd given her a simple wave when

we'd entered. We weren't close, but we didn't hate each other either. We'd been important to each other in the past, but that time was long gone. I was glad she had Nix now. Donovan, too. She deserved to be happy.

We stood when Miranski stopped in front of our booth. She had a file tucked under her elbow.

I extended my arm so she knew to sit first. She slid in and I settled beside her. Nix approached. He shook Cy's hand, then mine. Cy settled in the booth, Nix joining him.

"What do you have for me?" I asked, not eager for small talk. Not when Nix had sought me out.

Miranski set the folder on the table, opened it. "The fingerprints from Erin's house. I wanted to go through some of the names that popped up in the search. To see if you know any of them."

"To rule them out?"

VANESSA VALE

Nix shrugged. "Maybe, or if you don't know who they are, rule them in."

"Erin and I didn't run in the same circles. We weren't close," I advised.

Miranski nodded. "It's a small enough town."

True enough.

"There were Erin's prints. Kit's, too."

Nix nodded, well aware of his woman's connection to the murder. She'd been cleared, but until the real killer was found, some would wonder about her.

"Your parents' prints came up."

"They were closer than I was."

"A house cleaner who's been cleared."

The waitress came by, brought two glasses of ice water for the detectives. They declined any food and she left.

"Here are some other names. Tom Clinke."

MOUNTAIN DELIGHTS

I frowned. "Wasn't he a year behind us?" I asked Nix.

He nodded. "Works at the car dealership."

"I know him because we went to school together, but not how he knew Erin. Dated her, maybe?"

"That's what he said, but wanted your take," Miranski added. "How about Aiden O'Connell, Reed Parker or Mark Bastion?"

I shook my head, then paused, looked to Cy.

"Did you say Mark Bastion?"

Both Miranski and Nix perked up at my question. Miranski nodded.

"He's a ski coach," Cy said.

"That's right," Miranski replied after looking at her notes.

"I've never heard of the other two guys, but Mark Bastion is Hailey's coach."

"Hailey who?" Nix asked.

"Hailey Taylor, the downhill racer?" Miranski asked.

"And our woman," I said, looking to Cy.

"You found his fingerprints at Erin's house?"

"We did," Nix said. "What's up?"

"Mark Bastion knew Erin. Well enough to be in her house," I said.

"When would they have met?" Cy wondered. "Erin skied, but wasn't into racing."

I shook my head. "She liked picking out the cutest ski suit. She was definitely a slope bunny." I paused. "Wait. I told her about the mud run, the charity event up at Cutthroat Mountain last month where I met Hailey. Erin could have gone. Met him there. There's no way she raced, not if mud was involved. She could have met him during the event itself when I was on the course. I was with Hailey, so she

MOUNTAIN DELIGHTS

wouldn't have seen them together either."

"That event was before she was killed, right?" Miranski asked.

"A week or so."

The detectives looked at each other. "Maybe they met on the mountain, came back into town, had a fling. Things went south."

"Holy shit," Cy said, pushing at Nix to get out of the booth.

"What? What's the matter?" he asked as he got out of the way.

"Hailey's with him now. He came here to take her to pre-season training, but she's telling him she's done with racing. She said he's pretty aggressive, and she worried about telling him she was quitting."

I stood, too, seeing where he was going. "Mark Bastion is on your short list of suspects in the murder of my sister. His fingerprints are at the crime scene.

And he's with our girl right fucking now."

Cy ran for the door, drawing lots of attention. I followed along with Miranski. Nix stopped to talk to Dolly, then came outside after us.

"Where are they?" Nix asked.

"My house."

"Follow us, we've got the light bar."

I ran for the truck, said to Cy, "That won't be necessary."

"Damned straight. Hailey's with a murderer. Holy fuck."

13

AILEY

I STEPPED BACK, brought my hand up to my face. I'd never been hit before, but I'd fallen down a mountain more than once. Hit my head, even with a helmet. The pain from Mark's strike was intense, but it was more the surprise of it that had me freezing in place.

"You're going to go get your shit to-

VANESSA VALE

gether. All of it because you're not coming back here 'til the season's over."

I took a step back, then another.

"Move!" he shouted.

I jumped, then did what he said, went into Lucas' room. I had no intention of obeying him, I was just glad he'd let me out of his sight. He'd never hit me before, never gotten this angry, but I'd known he had a hair trigger. Not like this though. God, who was this man?

My cheek stung, and I could feel it beginning to swell. I wasn't going with him. No fucking way. But I had to get away from him and it wasn't out the front door. I went into Lucas' bathroom, locked the door and climbed in the bathtub. Why, I had no idea, but it was the furthest I could get. I needed help, but fuck, my cell was in the kitchen!

"Hailey!" Mark shouted, then

MOUNTAIN DELIGHTS

banged on the door. I jumped and grabbed on to the shower curtain. "What the fuck are you doing in there?"

"Going to the bathroom before we go," I called back. "Give me a few minutes."

Maybe he thought I couldn't escape the bathroom. Maybe he thought the slap was enough to put me in my place. As if. The opposite, actually.

I couldn't cower in the tub. I climbed out, looked to the small window over the toilet. It had opaque film on it so no one could see in. No curtain. It was tiny, but I was small enough to get through it. Luckily, Lucas' house was only one floor. I turned on the water in the sink to muffle my actions, then flipped the latch and pushed up the sash. Fortunately, Lucas had replaced the original windows with new ones. They were better for pre-

VANESSA VALE

venting heat loss, and thankfully, opening and closing as well.

Climbing up onto the toilet lid, I reached my arms through, then my head.

"Hailey!" Mark shouted.

"Just a minute," I called back. Putting my hands on the outside of the house, I pushed off, getting the rest of my torso through the window. Angling to the side, I got my hips past, then I leaned down and put my hands out when I dropped a few feet to the ground in Lucas' backyard.

I popped up and ran for the side gate. Sirens sounded in the distance, then louder and louder as they got closer. I heard tires squealing to a stop as I came around the side of the house, watched as people ran up Lucas' front walk, guns out.

Shouting came from within.

"Where is she?"

MOUNTAIN DELIGHTS

I knew that voice. Lucas.

Oh god, they knew I was with Mark. But why the police? I hadn't called them.

I ran around to the front, and back inside. Everyone turned to face me.

"Hailey," Cy said, grabbing me and pulling me into him. He was closer than Lucas and got me first. Lucas joined him, stroked my hair.

"Where were you?"

"I... I went out the bathroom window."

A plainclothes policewoman came out of Lucas' bedroom. She had on jeans and a black turtleneck, a badge on her belt and a holster at her hip. "The house is empty, the door to the bathroom is closed."

She glanced to me.

"Why the fuck did you have to go out the bathroom window?" Lucas asked.

"He... he hit me. Wasn't happy that I was quitting. He was making me go with him to training."

Cy pushed me back from him enough so he and Lucas could see my face. Their looks changed from concerned to murderous in a split second.

Lucas spun on his heel and launched himself at Mark, who was standing in the middle of the living room in handcuffs. With his arms behind his back, he could only turn his head away in defense, but it wasn't enough to avoid Lucas' wicked punch. The force of it knocked Mark down and he fell onto the coffee table, then crashed to the floor with a groan.

Another detective grabbed Lucas, pushed him back. Big, broad shouldered, dark hair. "Easy there, slugger."

"Nix, he hit my woman," Lucas growled. "And he fucking killed my sister."

MOUNTAIN DELIGHTS

The policewoman grabbed Mark's arm and yanked him to his feet, although he stumbled a few times on the way. His nose was bleeding, and he was breathing hard. His hair was a mess, and there was a tear in his pants.

"Kill your sister? Are you insane?" he shouted. "I didn't kill her!"

"You laid a hand on Hailey." Lucas jammed his finger into Mark's chest. "Show's you have no qualms with hurting a woman. Besides, you knew my sister. You were in Erin's house. Your fingerprints don't lie."

"I didn't *know* her," Mark replied, his smile tinged with blood. "We just fucked after the mud run event up at Cutthroat Mountain."

Lucas lunged again. Either the big detective was weak or he let Lucas hit Mark again. I was thinking the latter. With one well aimed punch, Mark toppled once more, right onto the coffee table with a grunt.

"Glad you skipped my dad and saved that shit up," Cy told him. "Nice hit."

A police officer came in the door and when the guy Lucas called Nix saw him, he hoisted Mark to his feet once more, pushed him his way. Besides the bloody nose, his eye was quickly swelling. He'd have a black eye within the hour.

"Book him for assault and murder," Nix said.

"He hit me. That bastard hit me with my arms behind my back."

"I didn't see anything," Nix said. "Did you, Miranski?"

"Nope. Just like he didn't know Erin Mills."

"Shit. Wait! I didn't kill Erin," Mark said, breathing hard and tilting his head to wipe the blood from his face onto his shoulder.

MOUNTAIN DELIGHTS

"We'll question you at the station after you're read your rights."

"I couldn't have killed her. I was in Canada."

Lucas stilled, glanced at Cy, then at me. Nix kept his gaze on Mark, studied him perhaps for deception. It was pretty hard to fake being in a foreign country. There were plane tickets to track. Customs.

I shrugged, not knowing my coach's schedule, only that he had been at the mud run. "It's possible."

"We'll check it out," Nix said. "Read him his rights before he says anything else."

The uniformed officer nodded, took Mark away while reciting the usual Miranda rights.

"Is your face okay?" Cy asked, turning me back to him, gently brushing his knuckles over the hot skin.

VANESSA VALE

"It's fine. I've fallen harder skiing than he can hit."

He didn't seem reassured by that statement because his jaw clenched.

"You think he killed Erin?" I asked, looking to Lucas. God, I'd let a murderer into the house? I'd been working beside one for years? I felt nauseated at the thought that I'd been in danger. "God, is it my fault they met? I was the reason he was at that mud run."

"Don't think that, doll. I'm the one who told her about the event. None of this is your fault. These are the detectives on the case. Nix and Miranski," Lucas said. They nodded my way as greeting.

"Do you need an ambulance?" Miranski asked.

I put my hand to my cheek. It was sore, but that was it. "No, it's fine. All I need is a little ice."

"His fingerprints were found at

MOUNTAIN DELIGHTS

Erin's. Miranski shared his name with us while you were meeting with him. It's possible he did it," Lucas added.

"He said he was in Canada," I said, repeating Mark's words.

Lucas shrugged. "Maybe all he did was have a fling with Erin and that's how his prints are there. He certainly has the hair trigger for the crime though." His gaze lowered to my cheek.

I'd heard they didn't think it was pre-meditated, but a crime of passion, of the heat of the moment. I wouldn't put it past Mark, now that I saw the real man. But if he really had been in Canada...

"We'll get to the bottom of it. When you're ready, come to the station and give a statement," Miranski said. "I assume you'll press charges?"

"She will," Cy said for me, his voice and tone I recognized as meaning there was going to be no sway.

VANESSA VALE

I nodded. I wasn't letting Mark get away with what he'd done. I might have quit, but he would go on to someone else, and I wasn't going to let him hit anyone else. "I don't like a bully."

Both Miranski and Nix nodded, then Nix slapped Lucas on the shoulder. "We'll get justice for Erin."

Lucas nodded and the detectives walked out the door, closing it behind them.

Lucas and Cy moved to stand in front of me, touching me, as if they couldn't get enough.

"I'm sorry," I said, needing them to know how I felt. "I was wrong... it wasn't just fun."

"Shh," Cy said. "Everything's going to be fine. We'll talk about it later. Let's get out of here."

"Yeah, I can't be here right now, not knowing what he did," Lucas added.

He walked off to the kitchen,

MOUNTAIN DELIGHTS

opened the freezer and pulled out a bag
of frozen peas, then pulled a dishcloth
from the oven door.

"Here."

"I'm sorry I stormed off yesterday," I
said, putting the cloth covered bag to
my cheek. I winced at the coldness. "I
was wrong, and I want you to know
how I feel. How I *really* feel."

Mark's break from insanity made
me realize what I had with Lucas and
Cy. How I'd been silly to push them
away. Selfish. I'd been afraid to fall in
love because it would hurt to have
my heart broken. But pulling away
from them, denying what I felt for
them, what we shared, was even
worse. I wasn't the only one with
issues.

Lucas had tons. PTSD that gave him
nightmares, or worse. Parents who
were mean and potentially insane. A
sister who'd been killed and a murderer

VANESSA VALE

on the loose. He needed me, and I'd pushed him away.

And Cy? His dad had abandoned him and it still affected him. He had epic trust issues, but he'd let me in, opened up to me in a way I figured he hadn't with anyone else. He was close with Lucas, but they were best friends. What Cy and I shared ran deeper. So much deeper. Why had I made him face his dad? If he wanted to avoid the guy who'd left him and his mom, and who'd so callously admitted to killing Erin, then that was fine with me. I should have understood, supported him, not tossed a butt plug at him and stormed off.

Now though, I wasn't keeping my distance. No longer. I was done running.

Lucas pulled me into his arms. "How do you feel about us, besides wanting to shove a plug up Cy's ass?"

MOUNTAIN DELIGHTS

I rolled my eyes at that because he seemed to be having similar thoughts as me. "I..." I swallowed, licked my lips and met Lucas' pale gaze. "I love you. From the very beginning, I think. From that first mud puddle. And you"—I turned to look at Cy—"since the skunk."

He grinned, the usually morose and serious guy appearing pleased. "Sweetheart, it was love at first skunk for me, too."

I smiled at that, remembering how awful it had been, how he'd taken care of me through it all. Leaning down, he gently kissed me. I felt the brush of his beard and wanted it elsewhere on my body.

But my sexy-times thoughts faded when he said, "I went to see my dad."

"You did?" I blinked back tears, thinking of him facing the man who'd caused him so much pain.

"Yeah. He didn't give me any answers, but maybe I wasn't really looking for any. I think I expected the guy from when I was nine to open the door. He's not the same man. I'm not that kid. I've moved on and he's now in my past where he left himself."

I didn't think it was that simple, or that he was completely over it, but he seemed content in his words. For now, that would have to do. I'd be there if it bothered him. It was my job to support my men.

Lucas pulled me in for a kiss. "You know I paid off your planned partner for the mud run so I could have you to myself."

I stared at him, remembering the first time I saw him when he'd introduced himself as my racing partner. Gym shorts and a T-shirt with his non-profit's logo across the chest. He was the hottest thing I'd ever seen.

I'd thought I was to be paired with a

MOUNTAIN DELIGHTS

Jamaican marathon runner, but one look at Lucas and I'd known he wasn't Jamaican, nor a serious runner. But I hadn't complained, not one bit. Not then, or a few hours later when he was soaping the mud from my body or after that when he made me come until I forgot everything but his name.

"You did?"

He nodded. "I put the Mills fortune to use paying him off."

I couldn't help but laugh. "Money well spent, in my opinion." God, he was everything. Cy, too, and that was scary.

"I'm afraid of being in love," I admitted, lowering the bag from my cheek. "I can't talk with frozen peas on my face."

Cy took them from me, stepped close and gently held them against my cheek. "You love us?" he asked, his dark gaze roving over my face as if looking for any doubt.

I nodded and the bag of peas rustled.

VANESSA VALE

"But I'm scared of what can happen. Of getting hurt again. I love skiing; it's my life, but one awful wipeout and it's over for me. I'm lost without it, or I have been. Until you. I want you both in my life, but I don't want you to *be* my life. And then, what if you drop me? What if I fall? That's why I pushed you guys away, why I tried to keep it casual. I can survive another knee injury, but my heart—"

"We won't let you fall," Lucas shared. "Your heart's safe with us, doll."

"Your ass, though, might get spanked though."

At Cy's warning, I couldn't help but grin. "Promise?"

"Hell, yeah. Now can we go to the ranch?" Cy asked. "I've got plans for you... and that ass."

"I don't want to stay here, not after what happened," Lucas agreed.

"Definitely, the ranch," I added. I

MOUNTAIN DELIGHTS

wasn't too thrilled to stay in Lucas' house, not after what Mark had done and not after climbing out the bathroom window. Even though Lucas and Cy would be with me, it was still too fresh. I was still running high on the adrenaline.

"Good," Lucas added. "Let's go. We both have plans for you."

"As long as those plans include you two taking me together, then I'm game."

14

Y

We left Lucas' truck at his house and rode in mine to the ranch. With Hailey's still at Mac's garage, there was no way she was getting away again. Not that I'd keep her like a creep, but for once, I was actually happy to be staying at the ranch. Avoiding people. Avoiding the world. But this time, not alone.

Lucas and I had the woman of

MOUNTAIN DELIGHTS

our dreams and we weren't letting her go. In fact, we were going to show her how much we loved her. Words were one thing, but actions were another. Especially what we had planned.

Hailey'd sat between us and it had been pretty fucking hard not to put my hands on her. But the bag of peas she held to her face was a reminder it wasn't time to get down and dirty.

We'd ensure she was okay, that she wasn't in any pain, then we'd take her, and claim her.

When we got through the front door, she dropped the bag on the floor and grabbed the back of my head and pulled me down for a kiss, I held off.

My dick wasn't happy, but she'd been slapped around. It could wait. We had all the time in the world.

"You okay, sweetheart? Headache?"

She bit her lip, her gaze raking over

my face as if it had been months and not a day since she'd had me last.

"I'll be fine if you fuck me."

I glanced at Lucas, who shook his head and grinned.

I took a deep breath, let it out. Ah, the sass on Hailey. I loved it. I loved *her*.

"Who decides if you get fucked?"

She pursed her lips. "You guys do."

I ran my hand over my beard, considered. "That's right. Maybe we'll sit on the couch, pull out our dicks and rub one out while we watch you play with your pussy."

Her mouth fell open. "You want to watch each other *masturbate?*"

"If it keeps your head from hurting."

She cocked her head to the side, then glanced down at the front of my pants. "No way you want to use your hand when you have me to fuck."

I groaned, then ran my hand down my face. This time, it was because she

MOUNTAIN DELIGHTS

was right, because she was so fucking in my face about it all.

"You're itching for a spanking, aren't you?"

She shook her head slowly. "Nope, I'm hoping to get fucked."

Lucas came up to her. "Jesus, doll. You sure?"

She looked between us, nodded.

That was all it took. Lucas beat me to it, bending down and tossing her over his shoulder. I followed him into my bedroom, watched as he tossed her onto the bed.

"If you like those clothes, get them off, otherwise they're going to be ruined," I told her, tugging the tails of my shirt from my jeans. I went over to the bedside table, opened the drawer and pulled out the small bottle of lube, tossed it on the bed.

She paused kicking off her shoes as she stared at it, then moved even faster.

Yeah, she wanted it.

She was naked and kneeling on the bed before us before I even unbuckled my belt. I paused and just stared.

"How are we going to do this?" Lucas asked me.

I took in Hailey's upturned breasts, the plump nipples hardening as we watched. Her breathing was ragged and they lifted with each quick intake. With her knees parted, we could see the slick folds of her pussy, eager and plump and ready.

"Gotta get her nice and ready to take us together. You want that, sweetheart? Me in your ass, Lucas in your pussy?"

She looked between us, nodded, her hair sliding long over her shoulders and down her back.

"Then we've got to get you nice and ready."

"I'm ready," she said, sliding a hand

MOUNTAIN DELIGHTS

between her thighs. "See?" She lifted it, showed that she was wet.

Lucas swore.

"What day is today?"

She frowned, confused. "Tuesday."

I glanced at Lucas. "She's not ready. She can still think."

Lucas grinned, stepped close and kissed her. "If you can remember more than your name, you're not ready. Don't worry, we'll get you there."

He pushed her down on the bed, climbed over her, keeping their mouths locked together. He played with her breasts, licked down her neck, took her nipples one after the other into his mouth. I watched him work her up as I stripped. As he settled between her thighs and got his mouth on that sweet pussy, I began to stroke my dick, gripping the base and working it, not going fast enough to come, but enough to hold me over until I had my turn.

Lucas could make her come like this, and we weren't in the mood to tease. He'd get her off so we could move on to getting her between us.

She needed to be mindless, wild with her need to get our dicks in her. Only then would she be able to take both of us at the same time. We were both big and it wouldn't be easy if she weren't aroused enough. Mindless.

"Lucas!" she cried, her fingers tugging at his hair.

I was going to come, just watching her get eaten out. The way she writhed, the way her head was tossed back. The look on her face as she came, the sounds she made, the way her skin flushed a gorgeous pink.

Fuck... I squeezed the base of my dick.

Lucas lifted his head, wiped his mouth with the back of his hand.

"What day is it?" he asked.

MOUNTAIN DELIGHTS

"Huh?" Hailey asked, not opening her eyes.

He pushed himself up, started working off his pants. He tipped his head to the side, indicating it was my turn.

"Hands and knees, sweetheart."

She didn't move, so I grabbed a pillow from the top of the bed then helped her roll over. Lifting her up, I slid the pillow beneath her hips. Ass up, head down, she looked gorgeous. She turned her head, blinked her eyes open.

"You still want us in you at the same time?" I ran my palm over her perfect ass, caressed the silky skin. I couldn't wait to get my dick inside as I held on, watched every inch of it disappear.

"Yes," she replied, the one word soft and almost slurred.

Lucas had done a good job getting our girl warmed up.

I grabbed the lube, flipped open the

top. With one hand, I parted her ass so the slick liquid dribbled down onto her virgin opening. I watched it tighten at the contact.

After setting the bottle on the bed, I slid my fingers over her folds, played with her pussy. I knew she was sensitive from Lucas' mouth, and I could get her to come again pretty fast. Her clit was a hard little pearl just aching for more love.

It would get it, but I'd get her ass ready at the same time.

With a finger at her back entrance, I worked the lube in, then the tip of my finger. The way she writhed on the pillow as I played with her pussy with one hand, her ass with the other, she liked it. A lot.

It didn't take long to get my finger all the way up in her, then I began to fuck both her holes, ensuring that my

MOUNTAIN DELIGHTS

thumb worked her clit, getting her off not once, but twice like this.

"Cy!" she screamed, gripping the quilt as if she might fly away.

"She's ready," I said to Lucas.

He moved to sit on the side of the bed, feet on the floor. I lifted a limp, sweaty Hailey onto his lap so she straddled him.

"Knee okay?" he asked, stroking her hair back from her face. I could see why he liked to braid it, but I wasn't taking the time now to put it up.

"Yeah," she whispered.

He kissed her, then lifted her up, got her in position over his dick, then lowered her down. I grabbed the lube and coated my hand, then spread it all over my dick as I watched.

He took her slow, let her get used to having him in her. Then he kissed her, pulled her down so he was on his back, Hailey lying on his chest.

With her knees spread wide around Lucas, I couldn't miss the way her little asshole winked at me, almost begging me to get inside.

Slick and ready, I tapped Lucas' ankle with my foot and he spread his legs wider, making room for me. Setting one hand on the bed at Hailey's hip, I gripped my dick, pressed it against her entrance.

Carefully, slowly, I worked it into her, easing up, then pressing more until she sighed. All at once, the head popped in. I couldn't help the groan at the tight, hot feel.

Hailey moaned and wiggled her hips, but didn't stop me.

I began to take her more, going deeper, inch by inch until we were both balls deep.

"You're perfect, Hailey," I said, leaning down so I could murmur in her ear.

MOUNTAIN DELIGHTS

"I love you both," she replied. "Now fuck me."

Ah, that growl, that sass.

I let my hand fall onto her ass, to give it a light swat. She clenched down, and Lucas and I both groaned. I gave up on anything but the feel of her.

Hailey came on a wail, her body stiffening, clenching and all but milking the cum from our balls. I wasn't going to last. What man could survive Hailey's gorgeous body?

It didn't take long for Lucas to come, and I followed soon after, buried deep. Emptying ourselves. Marking her. Making her ours.

But this hadn't been necessary to prove that. She'd always been mine. Always been Lucas'. We'd just been waiting for her.

We had her and we were never letting her go.

EPILOGUE

Hailey

IT HAD BEEN two days since the confrontation with Mark. Lucas and I were making dinner in the kitchen. I'd told him about my idea of leading some vet groups on ski trips, adding to his offerings. I wasn't a counselor and knew nothing about how to help anyone with any kind of psychological care, but I

MOUNTAIN DELIGHTS

could ski. I could be the guide and ensure everyone was safe and had fun.

He'd loved the idea and Cy had agreed it would be a great addition. Lucas and I had gone to the office, had phone conferences with the contracted psychologists, and plans for adding ski activities to the winter schedule were taking shape.

My life was taking a different direction, but I was excited. It held promise. Hope, and not just for me. I'd be helping others and doing it with the men I loved. It was real now, and it felt amazing. Fun. And by *fun* I meant falling more and more in love.

Cy came in from doing chores in the stable. He didn't give me the usual kiss I'd been expecting. When I turned to face him, I froze.

"What's the matter?"

He looked like the Cy I'd first met,

the rifle-toting, angry man who'd thought I was a hooker. Lucas lifted his head from the inside of the fridge, slammed it shut.

Cy dropped his cell on the counter. "My father's dead."

My thoughts swirled. Dennis Seaborn was dead.

"How... what... how?" I asked, sounding like an idiot.

"That was a lawyer in town." Cy ran a hand over his beard, shaking his head. "I'm next of kin. Hell, I'm the only kin he had."

"How?" Lucas asked.

"He had pancreatic cancer."

"Holy shit." Lucas let out a harsh breath. "I only saw him from the truck when we went to his house, but he didn't look sick, only... old."

Cy nodded in agreement. I'd only seen a picture on the news and it had

MOUNTAIN DELIGHTS

been a mug shot. He'd looked like a weathered, unhappy, late-fifties version of Cy.

"He had scheduled a Whipple procedure. I have no idea what that is, but some kind of surgery. He didn't make it off the table."

"Did he tell you he was sick?" Lucas asked.

"Not a word."

I went over to him, wrapped my arms around him, hugged him close. He might be big and brawny, but I'd learned he was vulnerable, too.

His hand settled on my head, stroked down my braid. "That's not all."

I pulled back, looked up at him.

"He left me three million dollars."

I stepped back, stared. I glanced at Lucas, who looked as stunned as me. As Cy.

"What the fuck?" Lucas whispered.

"That was my first thought," Cy said. "The lawyer said he'd come into some money recently. He'd set it all aside for me. The instructions were clear."

Lucas paced the kitchen, then slapped his hand on the counter. "You don't think—"

"He manned up," Cy said.

"I don't understand," I murmured, watching both of them carefully. While they looked confused, they seemed to know things I didn't.

"That's what he said to me when I asked why he'd admitted to killing Erin."

"He manned up," I repeated.

Cy nodded, running a hand over the back of his neck, then his beard.

"He knew he was dying and did it for you."

"What? Confessed to something he didn't do? But why?" I asked.

"Because someone wanted him to

MOUNTAIN DELIGHTS

take the fall," Lucas added.

I still didn't get it.

Lucas stared at Cy, who nodded.

"The money was wired into a special account from Mills Land Trust the day he walked into the station and admitted to the crime."

I held up my hand, stared at Lucas. "That's your family's company."

"Yeah," he replied, slowly shaking his head. "Who didn't hate your guts after what your father did?"

I thought of when we'd gone to Lucas' sister's house to help move. Mr. and Mrs. Mills should have hated Cy for his father's actions, for falsely admitting to killing their daughter, but they hadn't. Why?

"Holy shit. They paid Cy's dad to do it. They knew he was dying. But why?" I asked.

Lucas looked to me. His jaw was clenched, his hands in fists at his sides.

His usually calm pale eyes were a stormy sea. "The only reason that makes sense is that they fucking think I did it."

NOTE FROM VANESSA

Guess what? I've got some bonus content for you with Hailey, Cy and Lucas. So sign up for my mailing list. There will be special bonus content for books, just for my subscribers. Signing up will let you hear about my next release as soon as it is out, too (and you get a free book...wow!)

As always...thanks for loving my books and the wild ride!

NOTE FROM VANESSA

Vanessa

JOIN THE WAGON TRAIN!

If you're on Facebook, please join my closed group, the Wagon Train! Don't miss out on the giveaways and hot cowboys!

https://www.facebook.com/groups/vanessavalewagontrain/

GET A FREE BOOK!

Join my mailing list to be the first to know of new releases, free books, special prices and other author giveaways.

http://freeromanceread.com

ALSO BY VANESSA VALE

Wild Mountain Men

Mountain Darkness

Mountain Delights

Mountain Desire

Mountain Deceit

Mountain Danger

Grade-A Beefcakes

Sir Loin Of Beef

T-Bone

Tri-Tip

Porterhouse

Skirt Steak

Small Town Romance

Montana Fire

Montana Ice

Montana Heat

Montana Wild

Montana Mine

Steele Ranch

Spurred

Wrangled

Tangled

Hitched

Lassoed

Bridgewater County Series

Ride Me Dirty

Claim Me Hard

Take Me Fast

Hold Me Close

Make Me Yours

Kiss Me Crazy

Mail Order Bride of Slate Springs Series

A Wanton Woman

A Wild Woman

A Wicked Woman

Bridgewater Ménage Series

Their Runaway Bride

Their Kidnapped Bride

Their Wayward Bride

Their Captivated Bride

Their Treasured Bride

Their Christmas Bride

Their Reluctant Bride

Their Stolen Bride

Their Brazen Bride

Their Rebellious Bride

Their Reckless Bride

Outlaw Brides Series

Flirting With The Law

MMA Fighter Romance Series

Fight For Her

Wildflower Bride Series

Rose

Hyacinth

Dahlia

Daisy

Lily

Montana Men Series

The Lawman

The Cowboy

The Outlaw

Standalone Reads

Twice As Delicious

Western Widows

Sweet Justice

Mine To Take

Relentless

Sleepless Night

Man Candy - A Coloring Book

ABOUT THE AUTHOR

Vanessa Vale is the *USA Today* Bestselling author of over 60 books, sexy romance novels, including her popular Bridgewater historical romance series and hot contemporary romances featuring unapologetic bad boys who don't just fall in love, they fall hard. When she's not writing, Vanessa savors the insanity of raising two boys and figuring out how many meals she can make with a pressure cooker. While she's not as skilled at social media as her kids, she loves to interact with readers.

BookBub

Instagram

www.vanessavaleauthor.com